P9-CQK-371

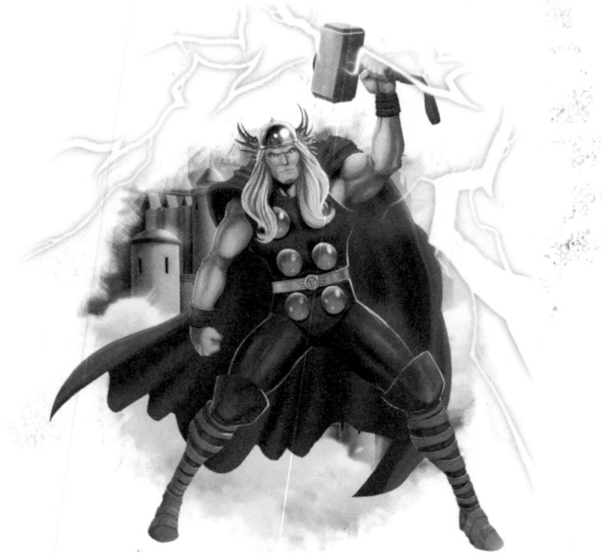

A GOLDEN BOOK • NEW YORK

 Published in the United States by Golden Books, an imprint of Random House Children's Books, a division of Penguin Random House LLC, 1745 Broadway, New York, NY 10019, and in Canada by Penguin Random House Canada Limited, Toronto. The stories contained in this work were originally published as *The Mighty Avengers* in 2012; *Lights Out!* in 2013; and *Thunder Strike!* in 2017. Golden Books, A Golden Book, A Little Golden Book, the G colophon, and the distinctive gold spine are registered trademarks of Penguin Random House LLC.

rhcbooks.com

ISBN 978-0-525-57786-7

MANUFACTURED IN CHINA

10 9 8 7 6 5 4 3 2 1

MARVEL

AVENGERS

THE MIGHTY AVENGERS

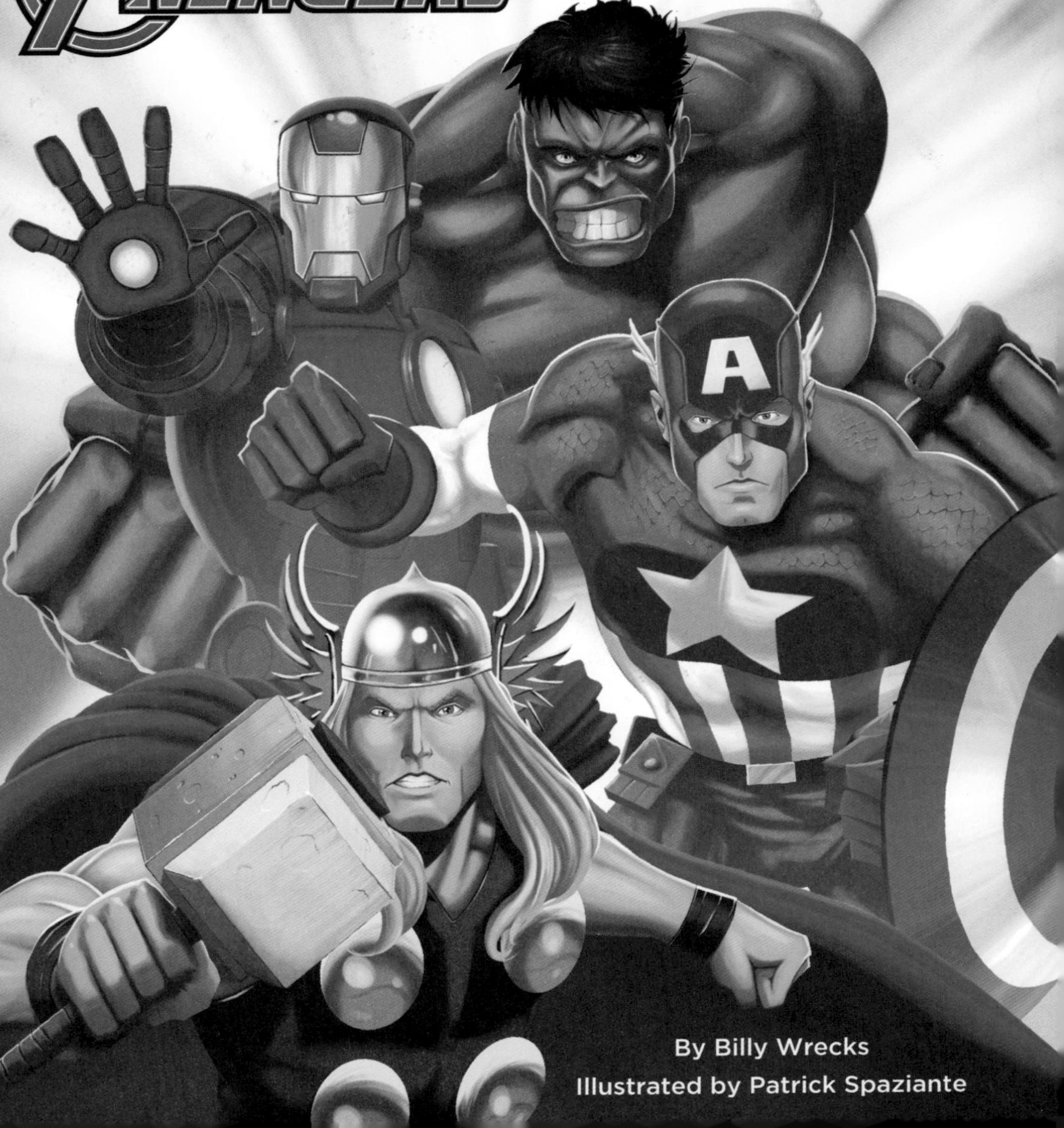

By Billy Wrecks

Illustrated by Patrick Spaziante

When Earth is in great danger, the world's mightiest super heroes assemble. Together they are known as . . .

The Avengers!

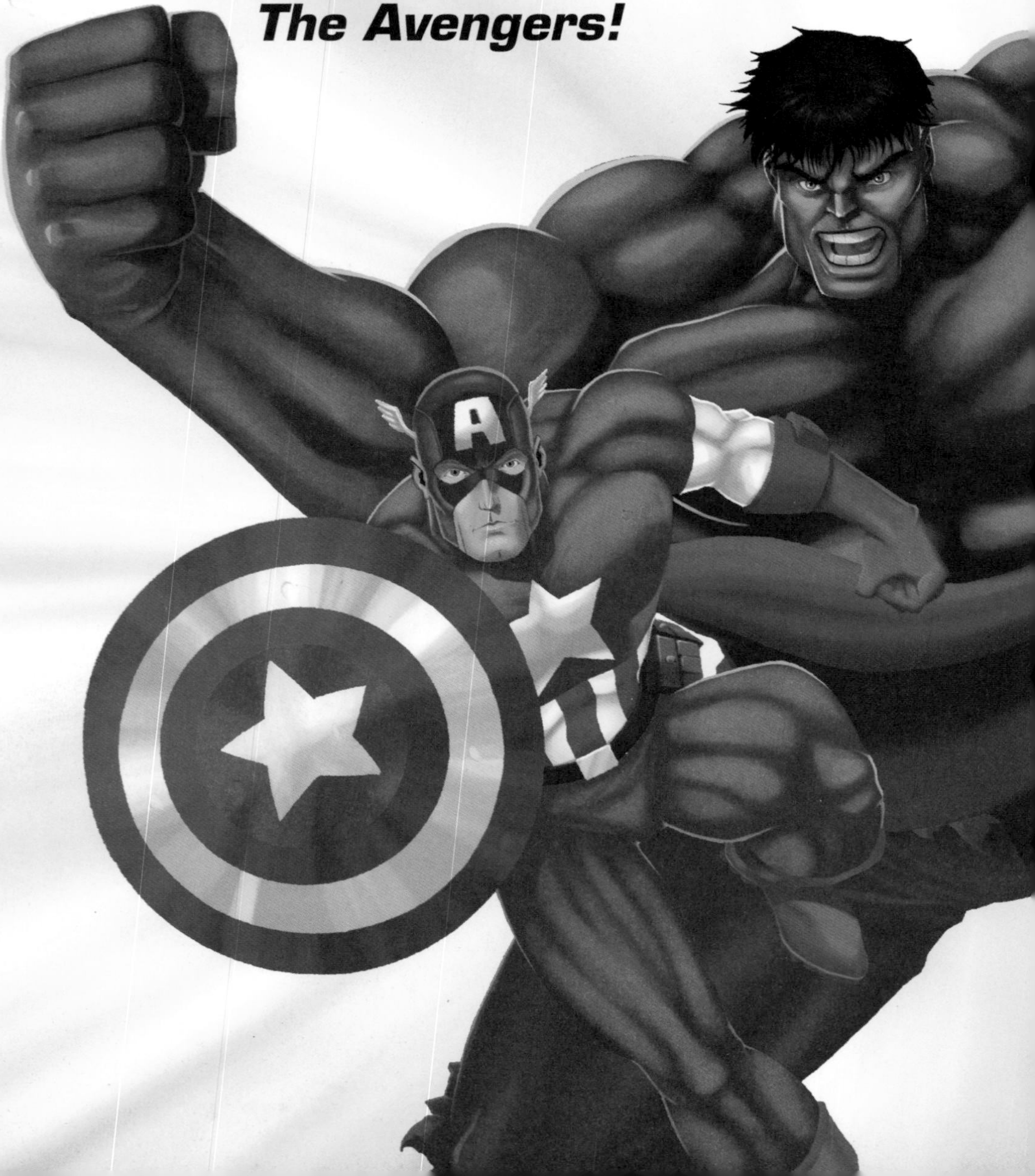

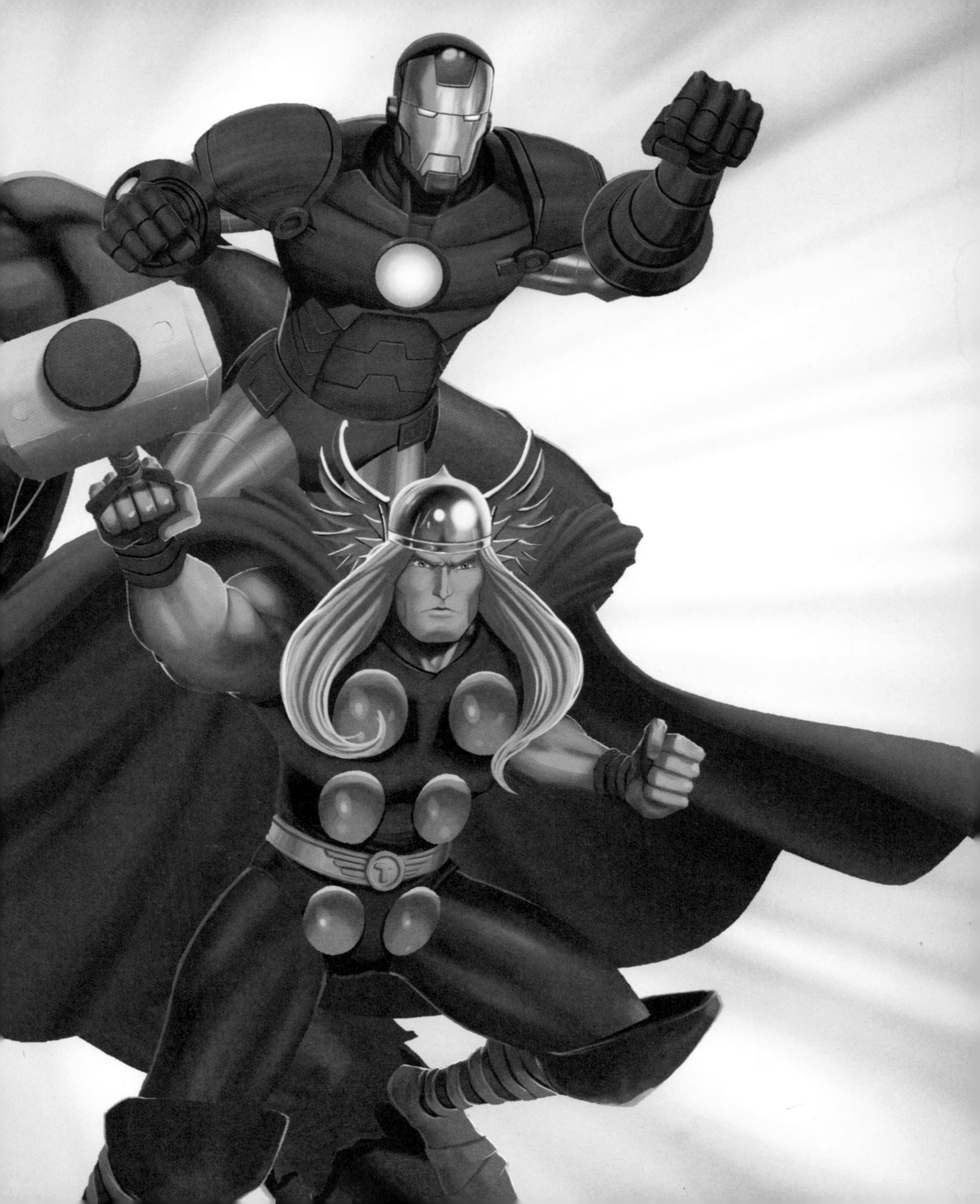

Captain America!

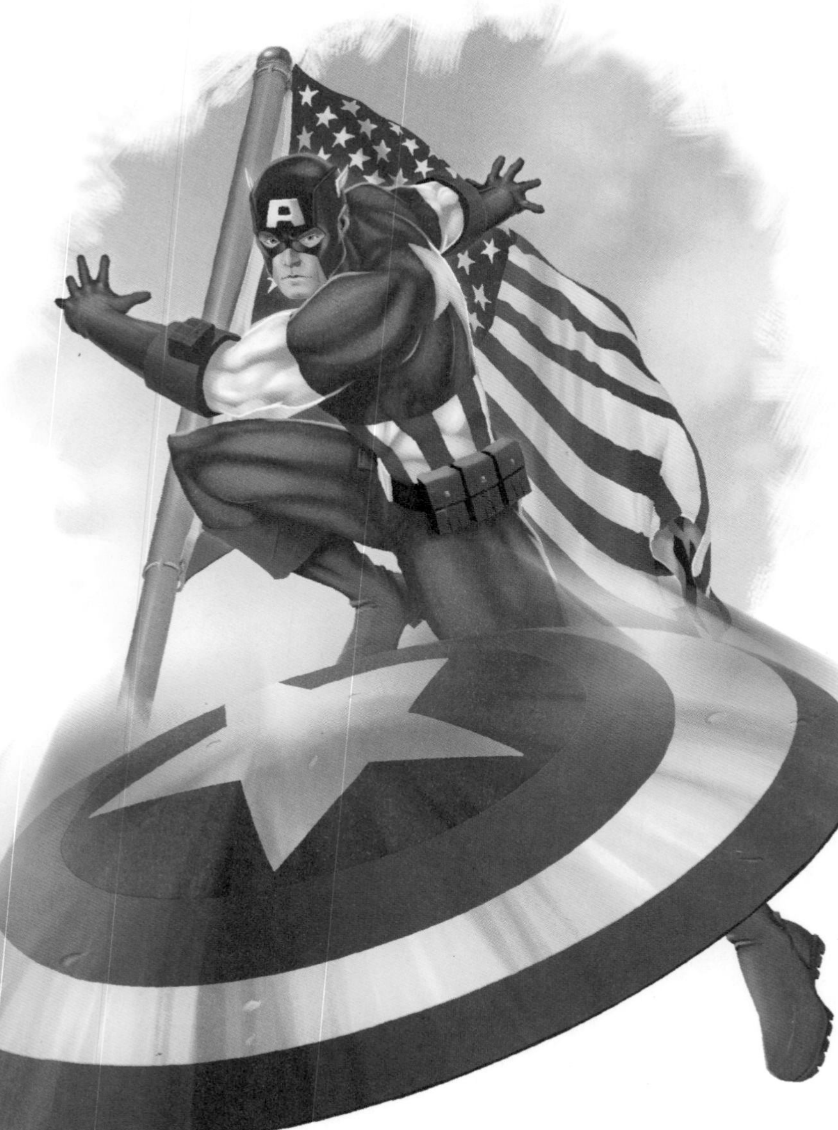
A

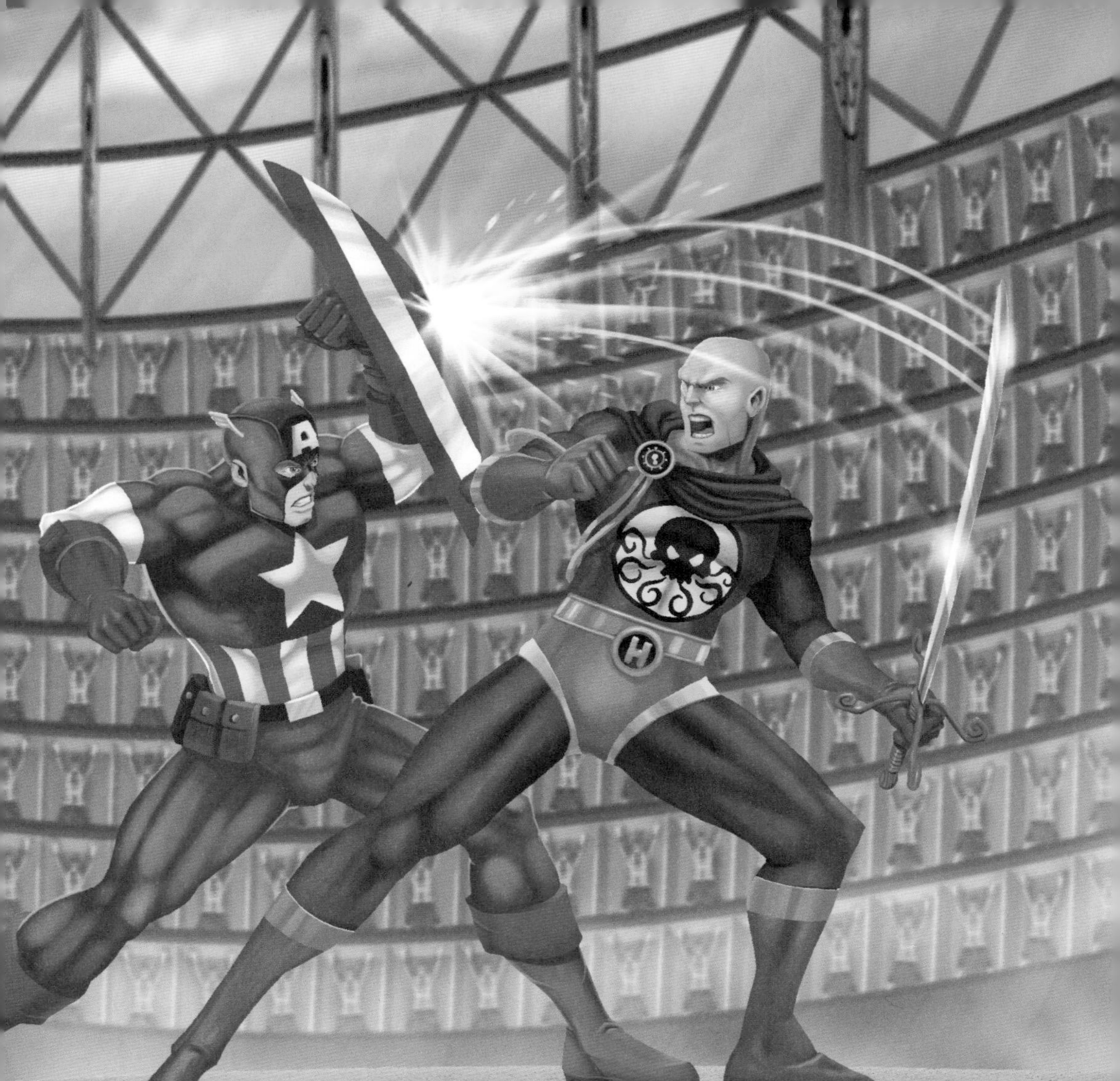

Captain America has the strength and speed of a great athlete. With his unbreakable shield, Captain America leads the Avengers in their never-ending fight to defend truth, justice, and freedom.

Iron Man!

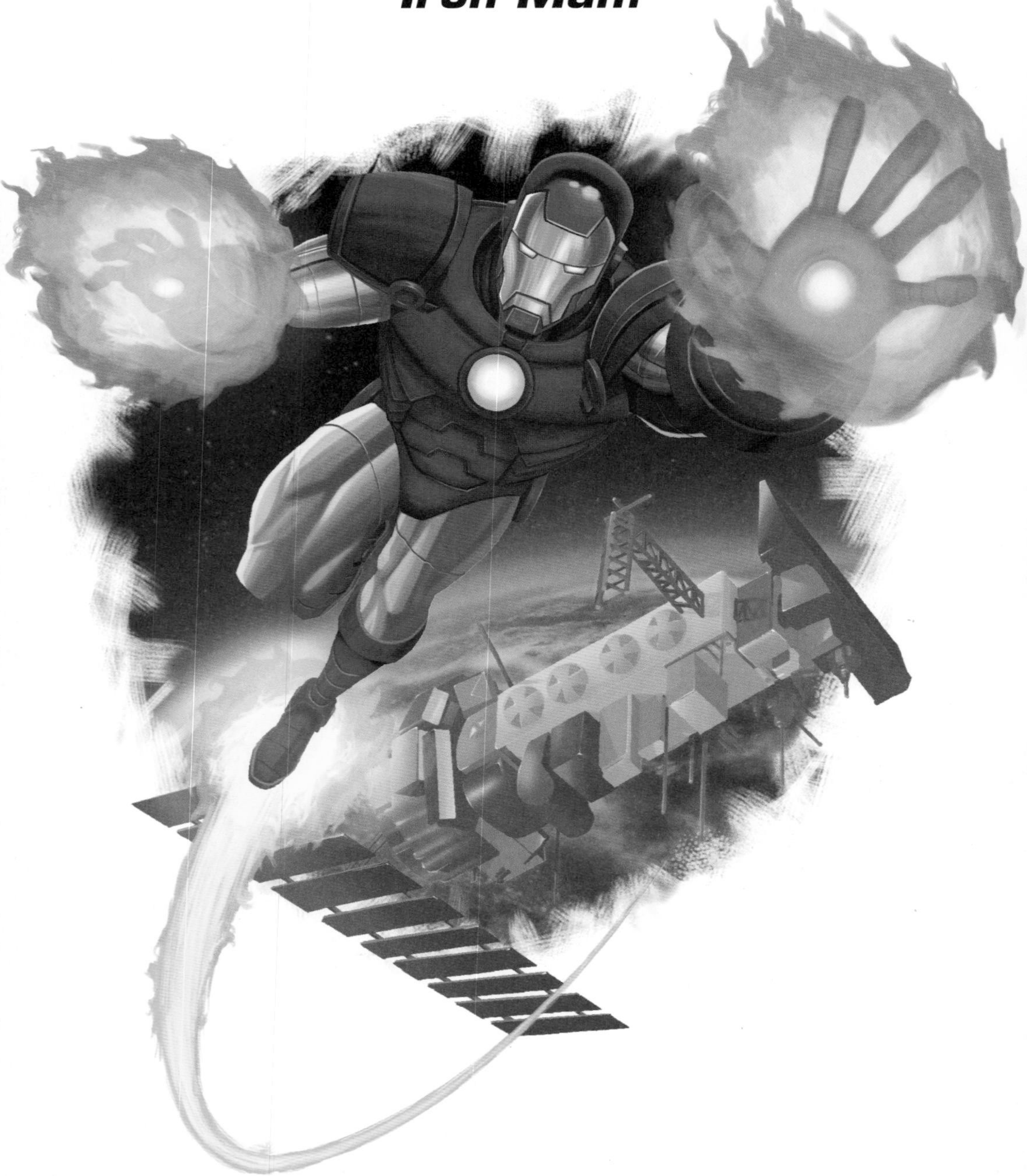

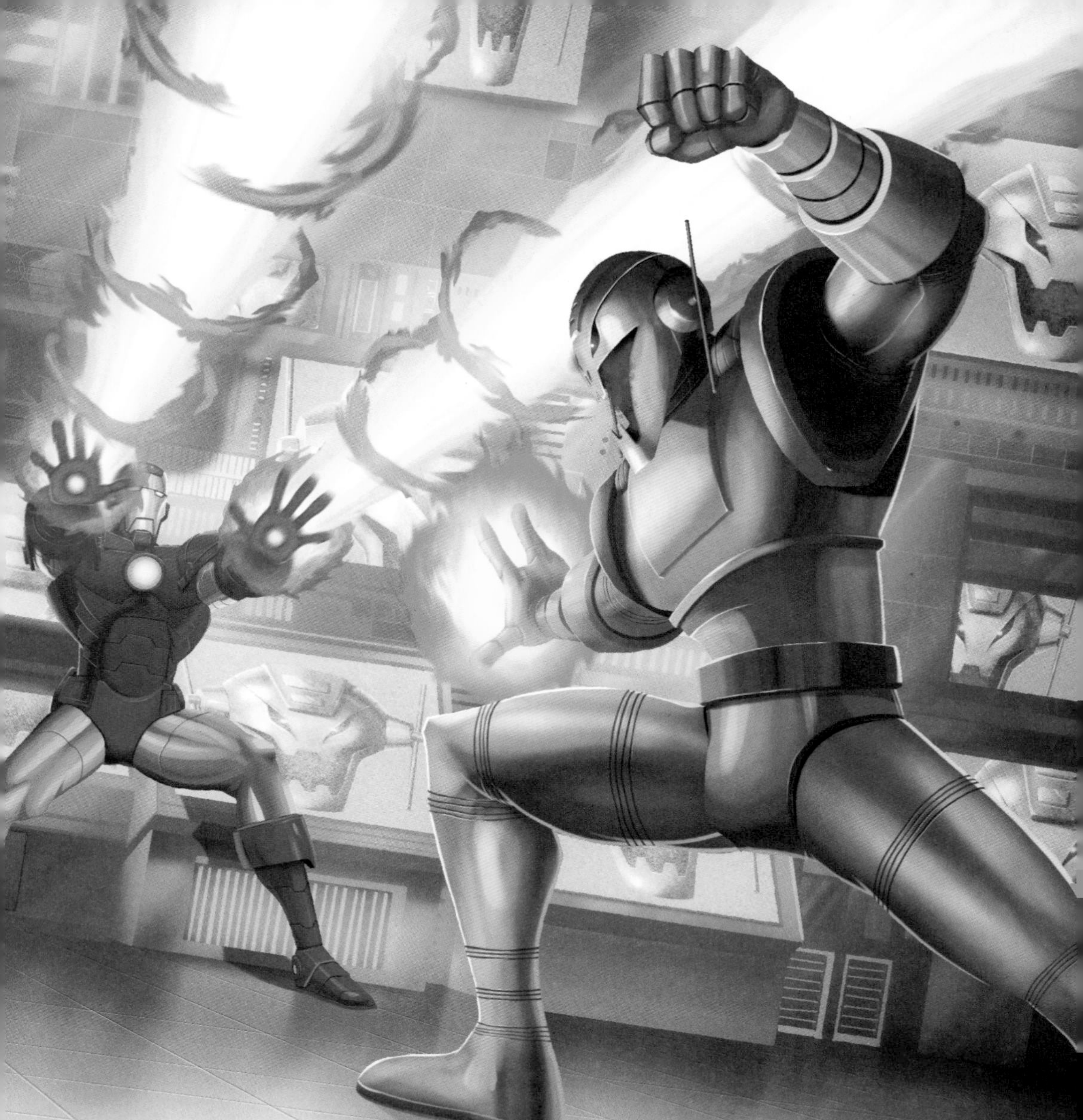

Iron Man wears armor that allows him to fly and fire powerful repulsor rays! Iron Man keeps the Avengers one step ahead of the super criminals who use advanced technology for their far-reaching plots.

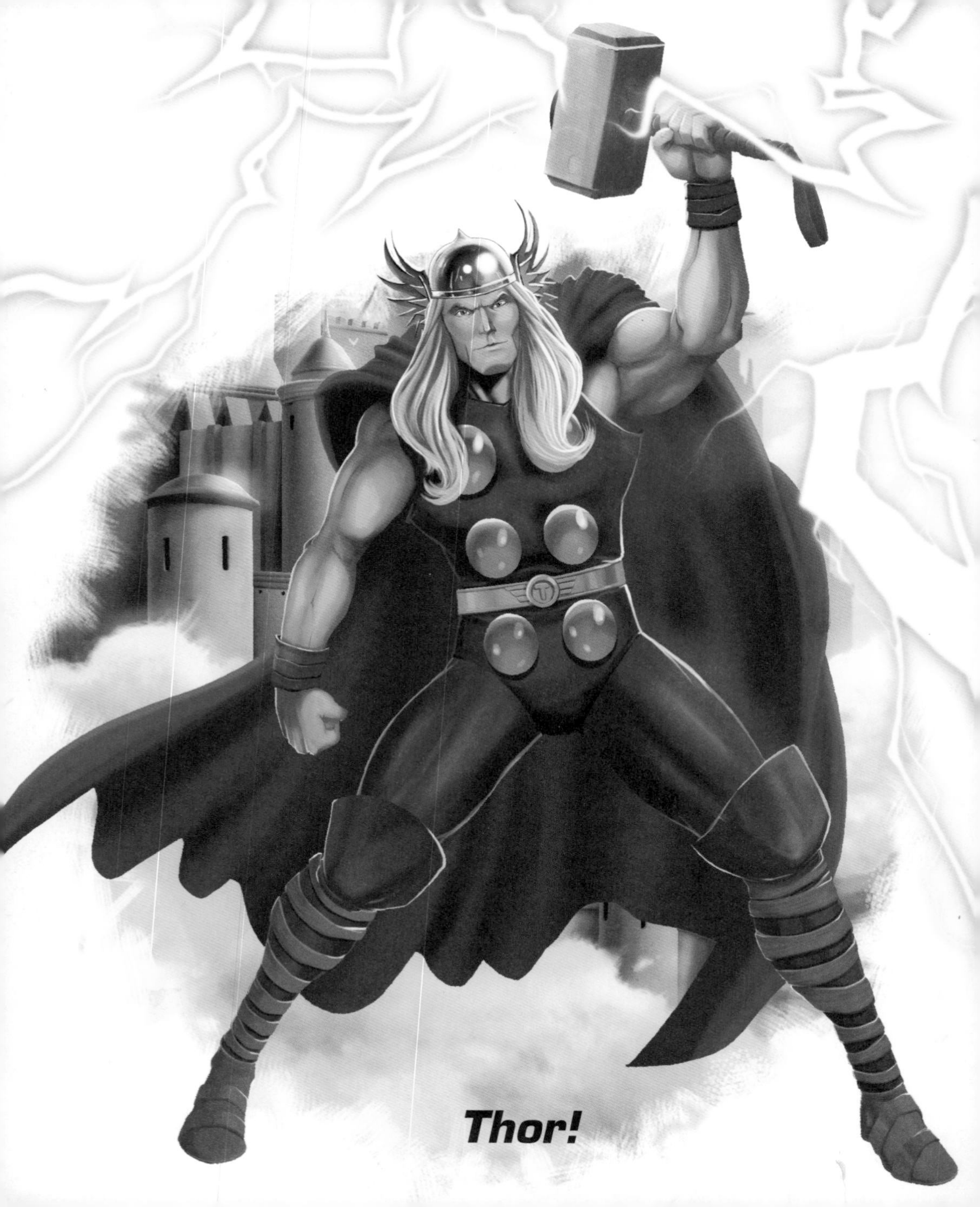

Thor!

Thor can control wind, rain, and lightning! When he spins his magical hammer, Thor can fly through the air at amazing speeds.

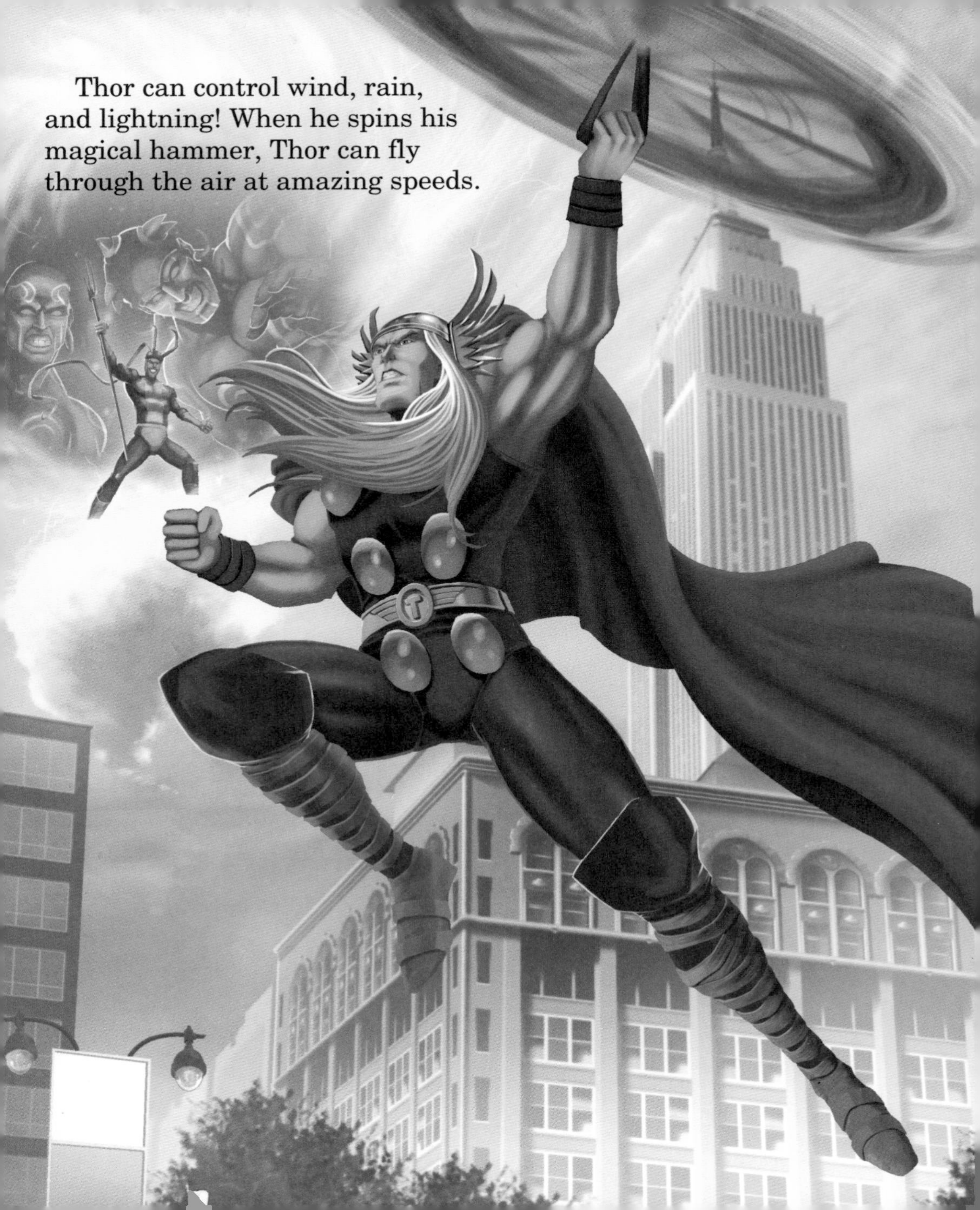

Hulk!

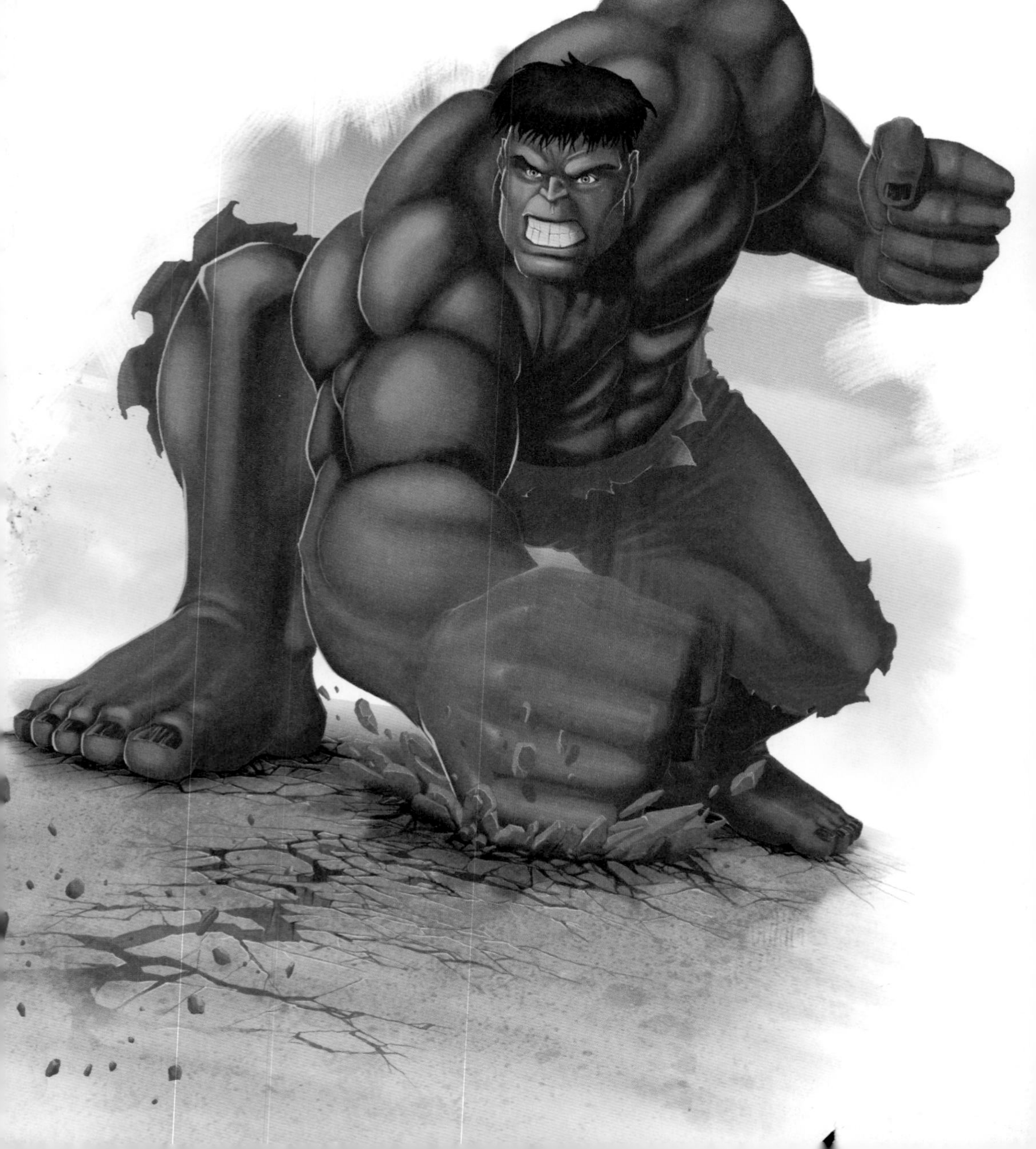

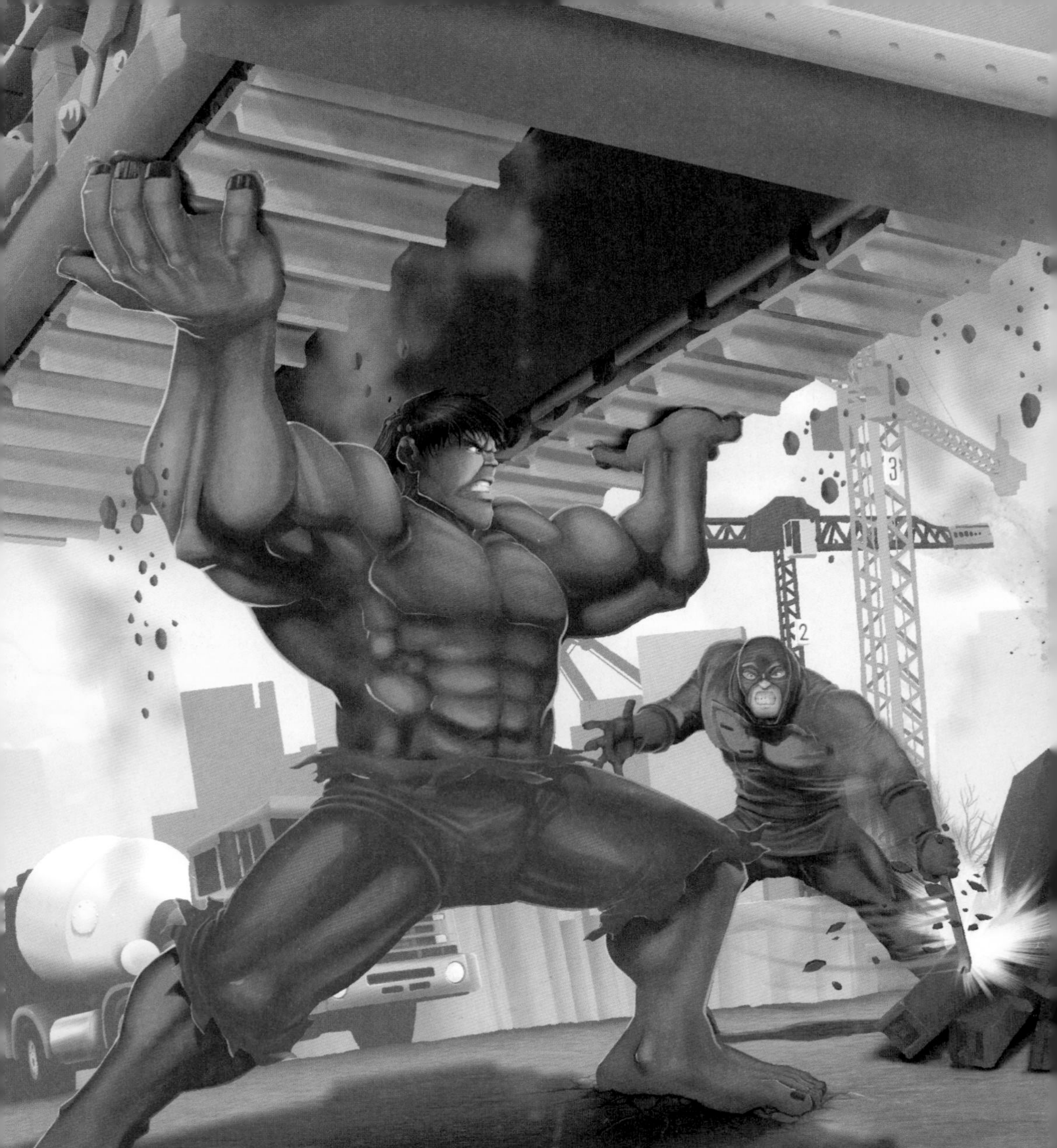

Hulk is the strongest hero there is! When the Avengers must face one of their toughest enemies, Hulk is the green-skinned giant for the job.

The criminal organization called **HYDRA** wants to take over the world! But they will never succeed, because the Avengers will always stand in their way.

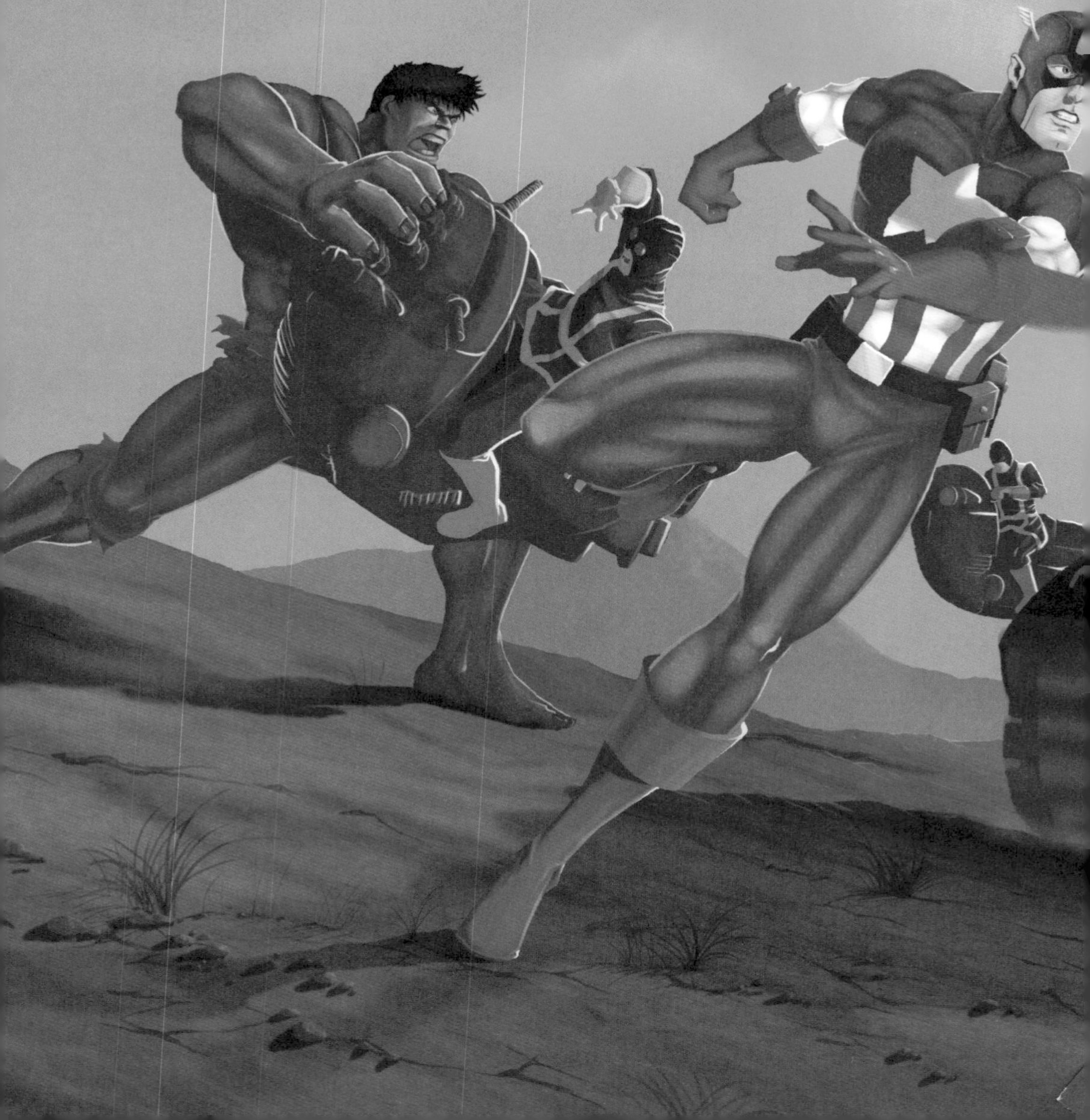

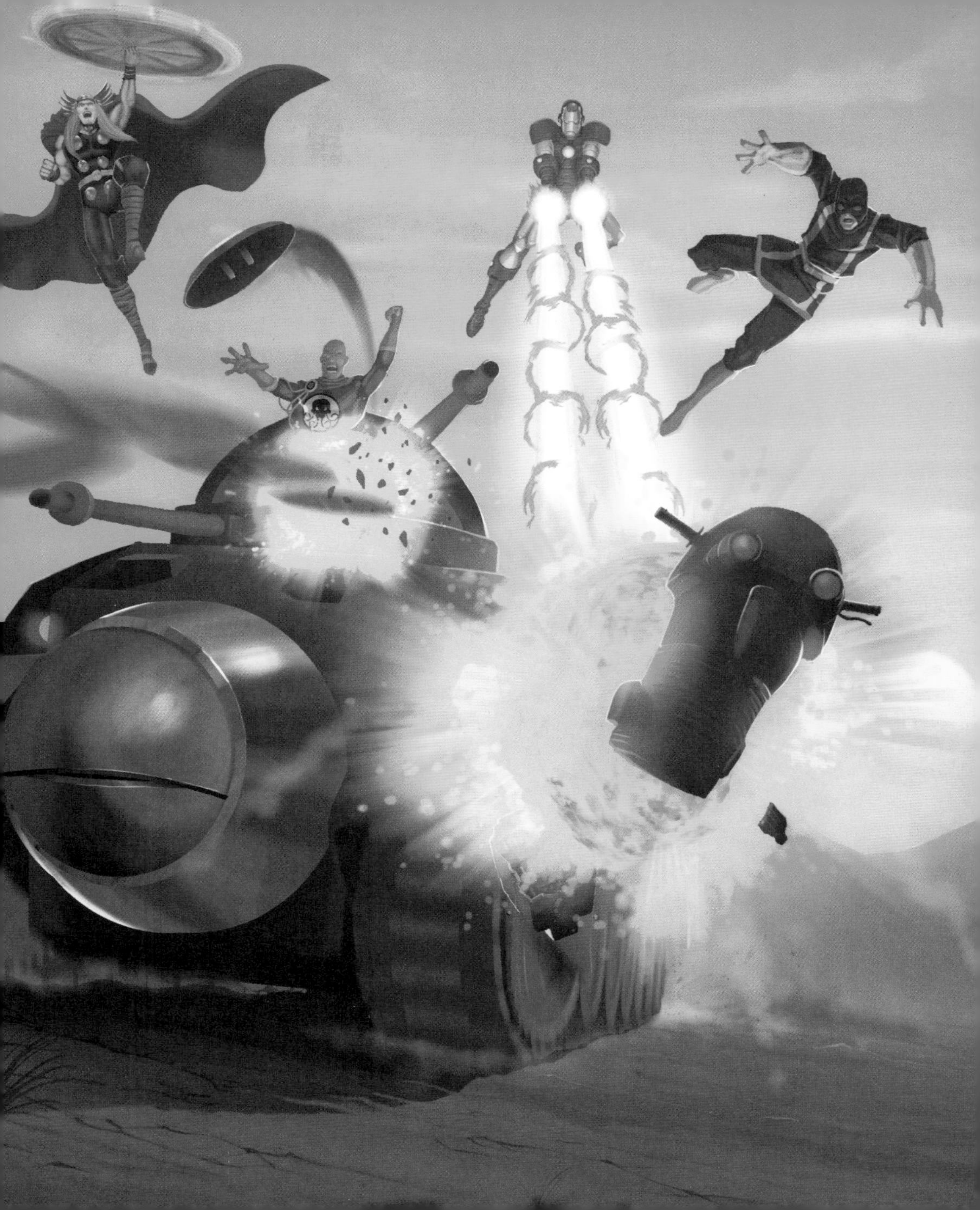

The **Wrecker** and the Wrecking Crew are superstrong bullies who think they can take whatever they want, whenever they want it! Luckily, the Avengers have the courage to take them on—any time and any place!

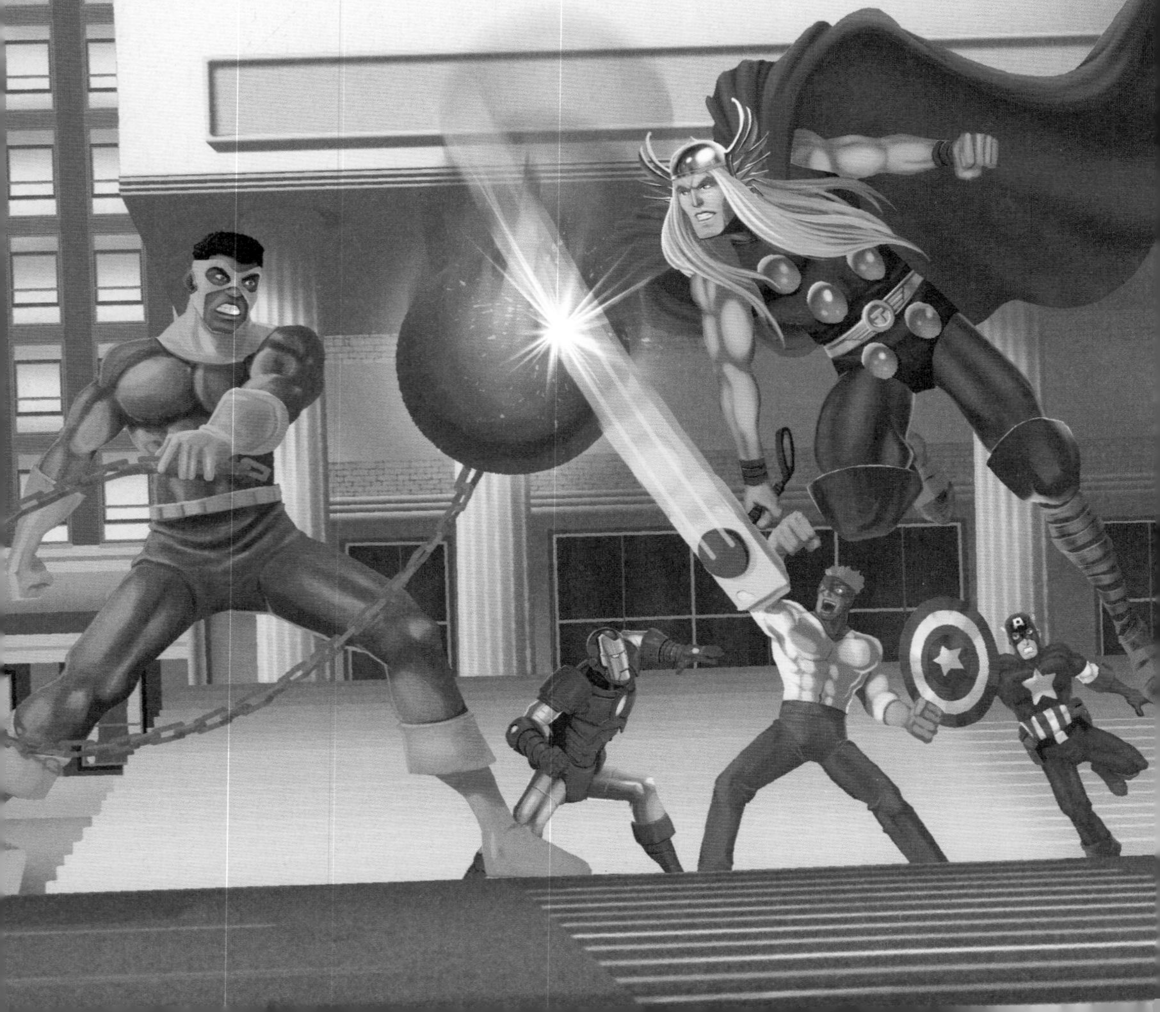

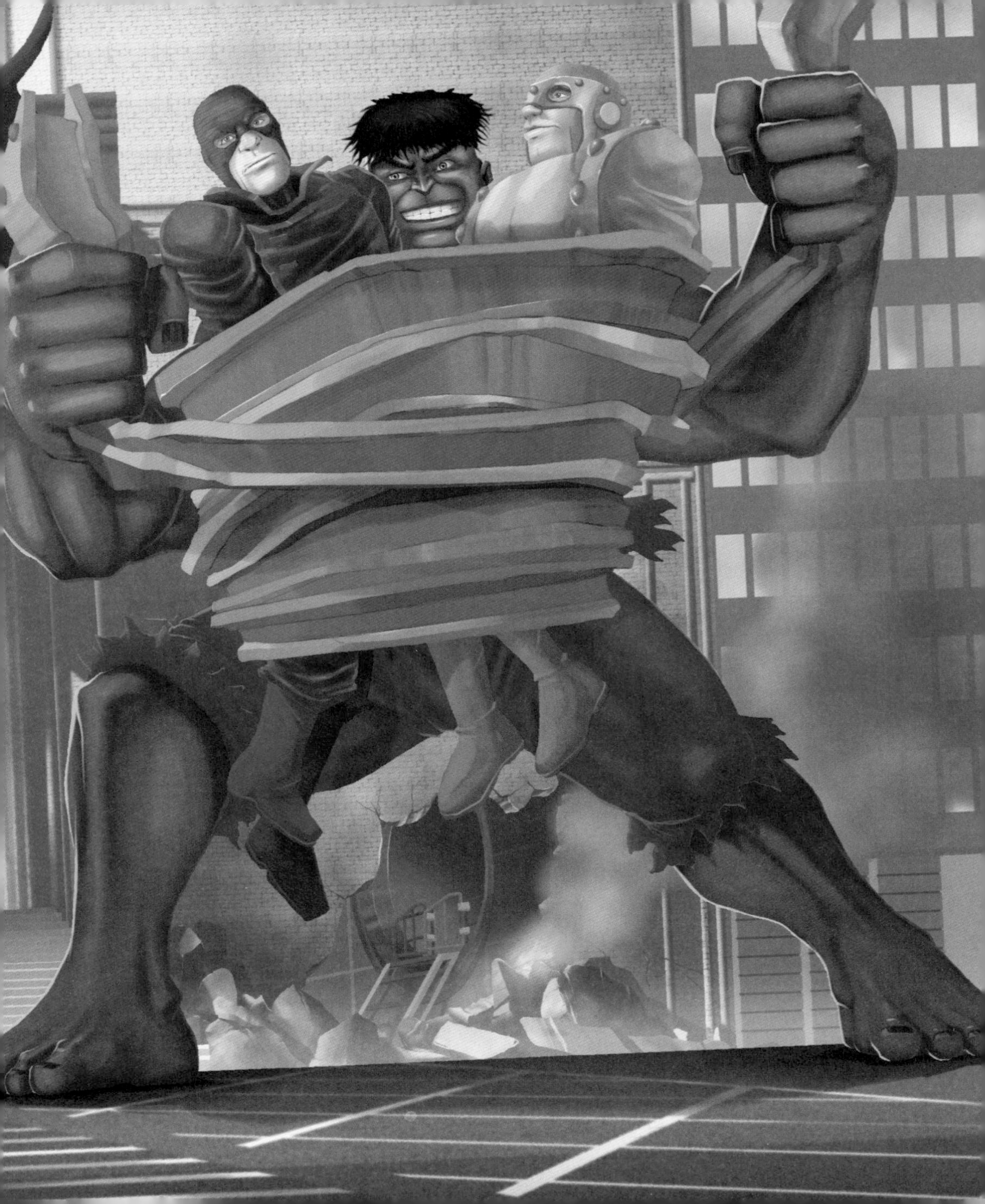

Thor's evil brother, **Loki,** uses magic to try to get his wicked way. Luckily, neither magic nor sinister schemes can overcome the combined courage of the Avengers!

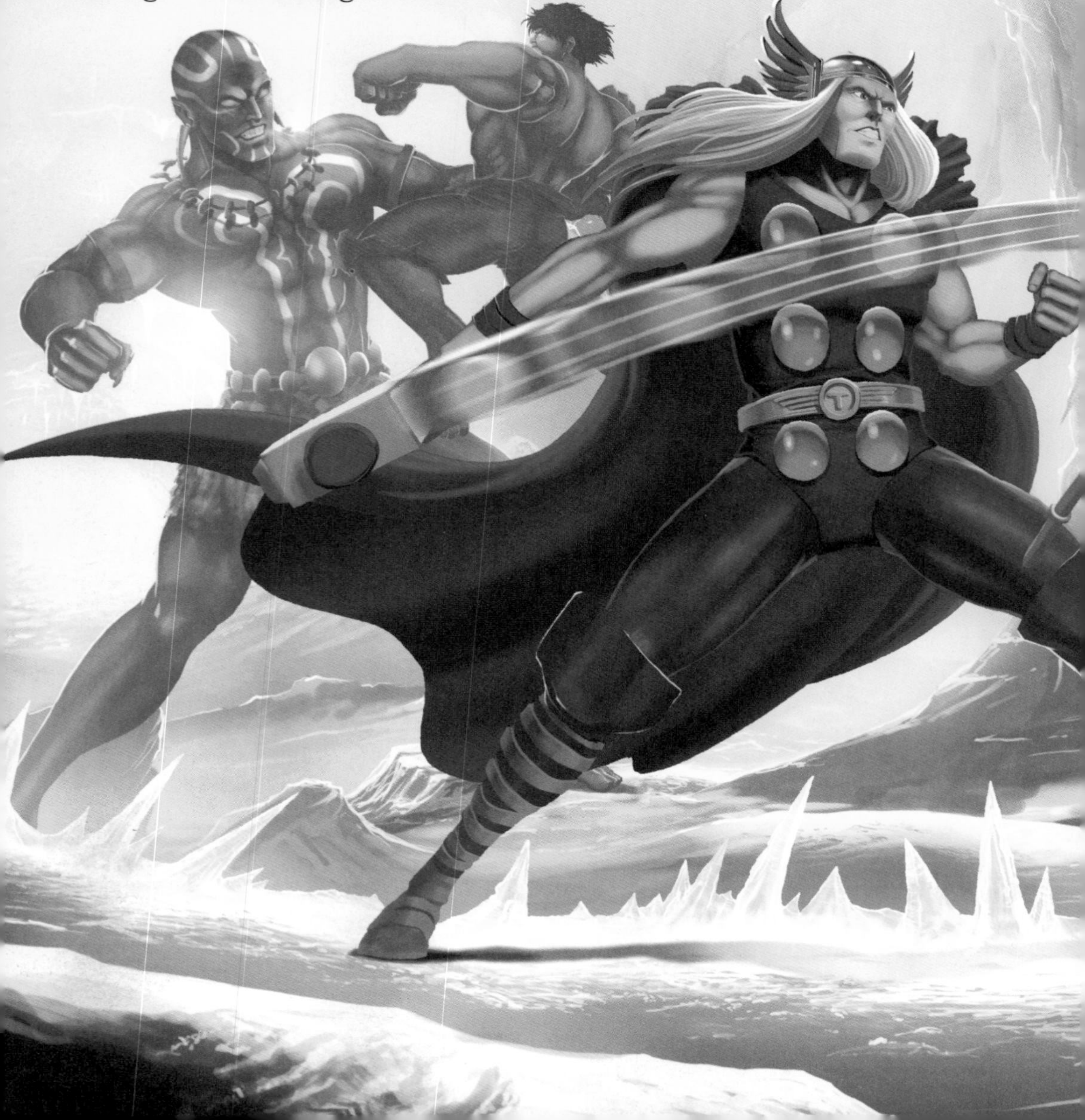

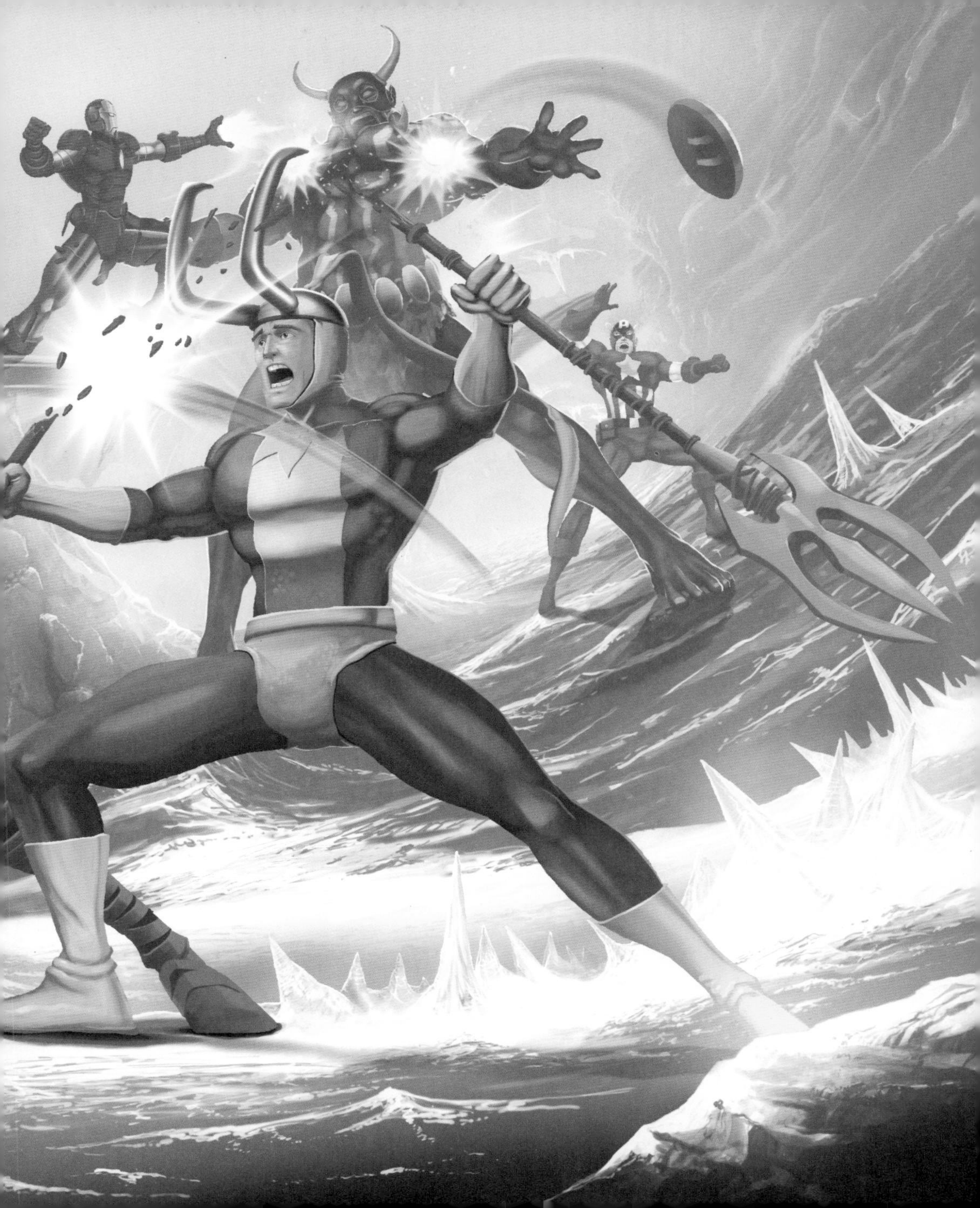

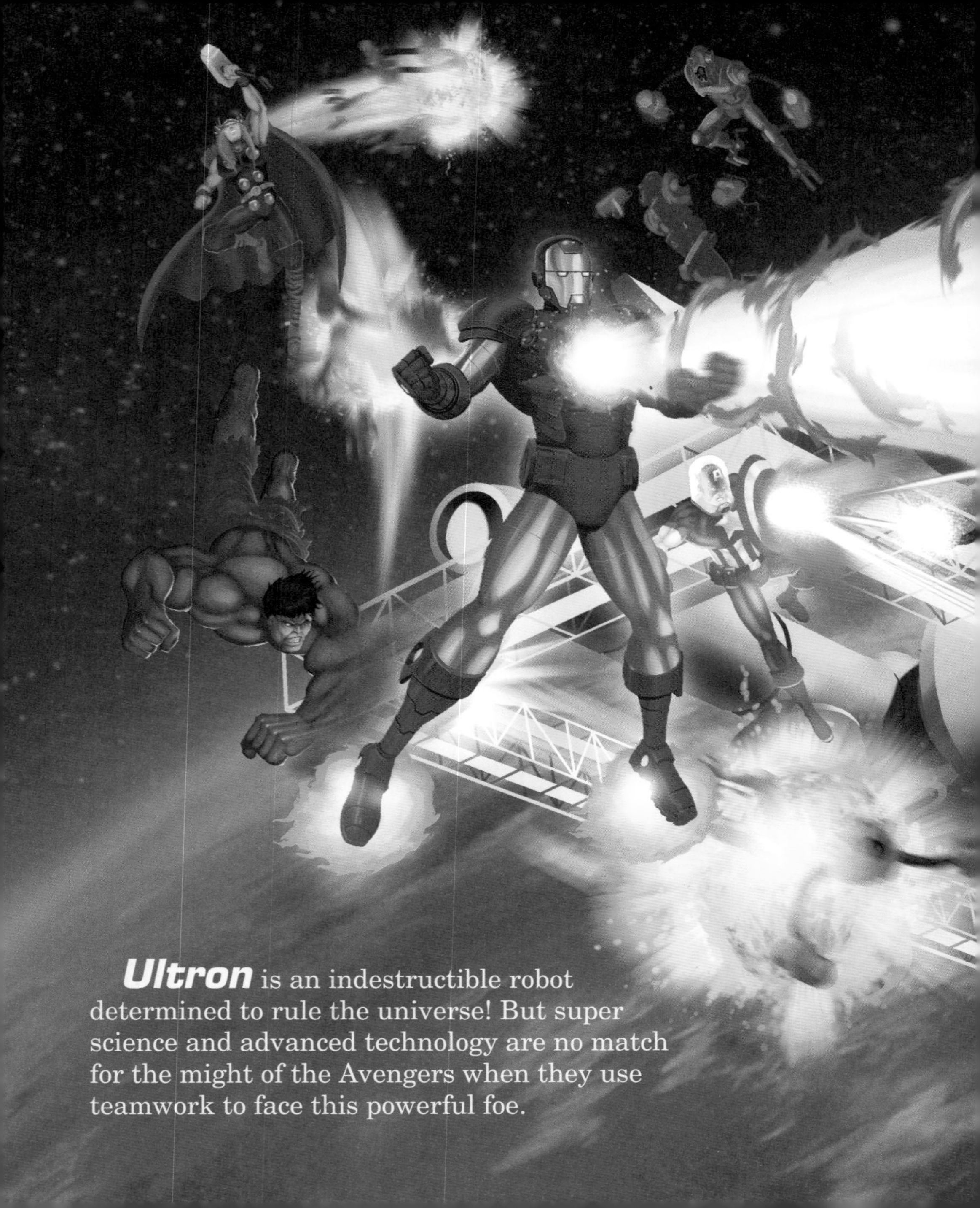

Ultron is an indestructible robot determined to rule the universe! But super science and advanced technology are no match for the might of the Avengers when they use teamwork to face this powerful foe.

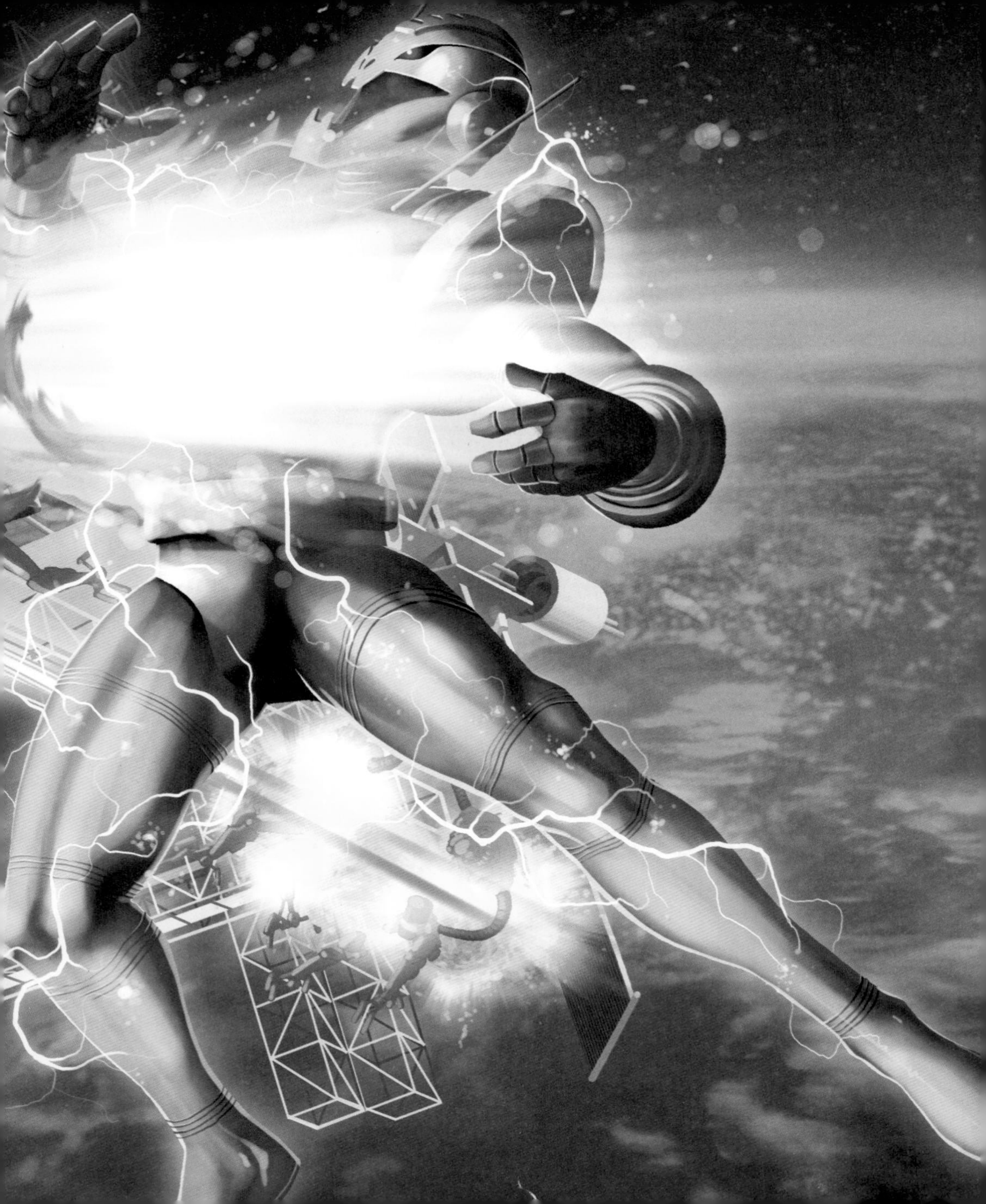

After stopping the bad guys, the Avengers take them to a high-tech prison called the ***Vault***. Locked away, the villains can do no more harm—but they're always looking for a way to escape!

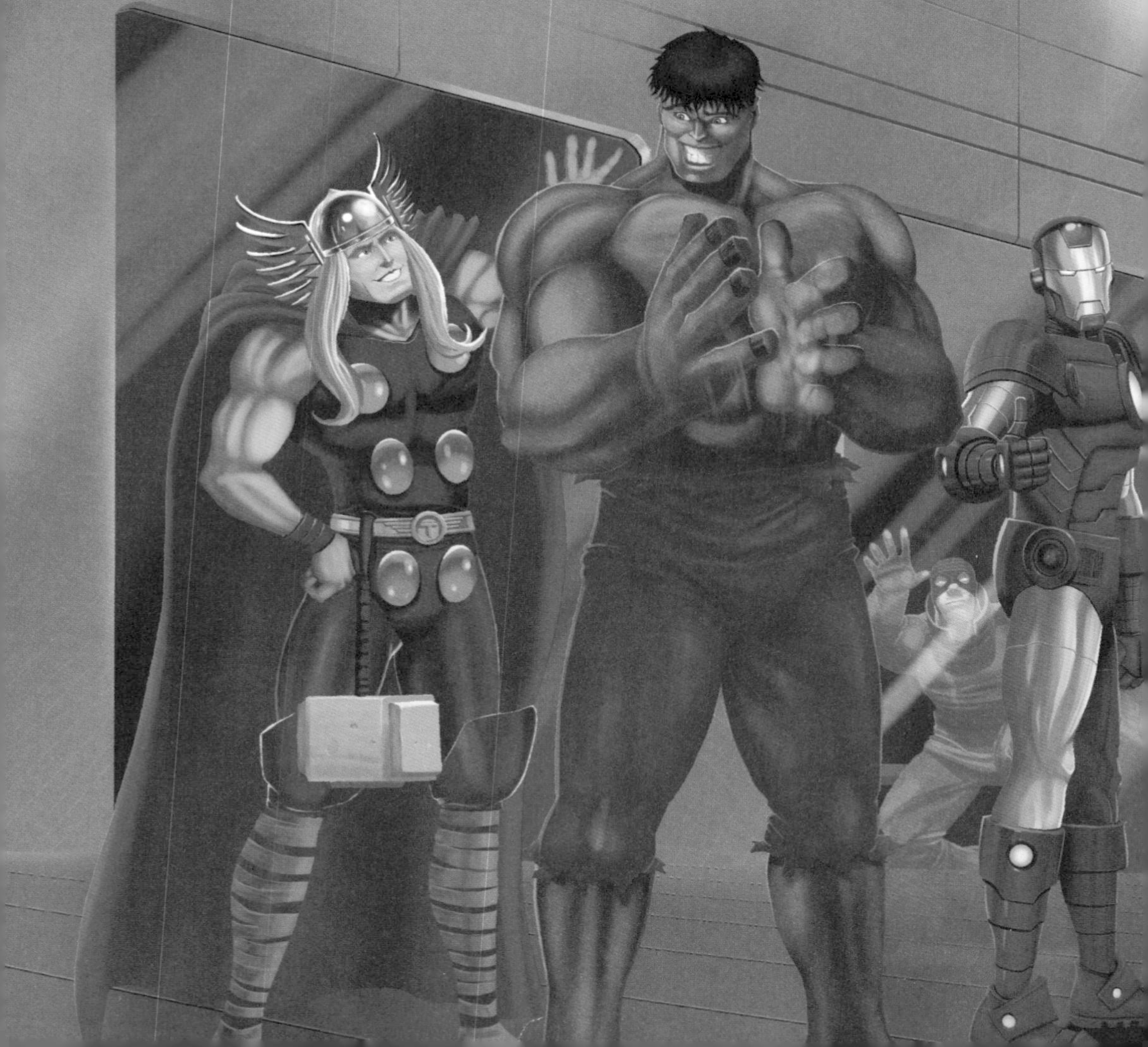

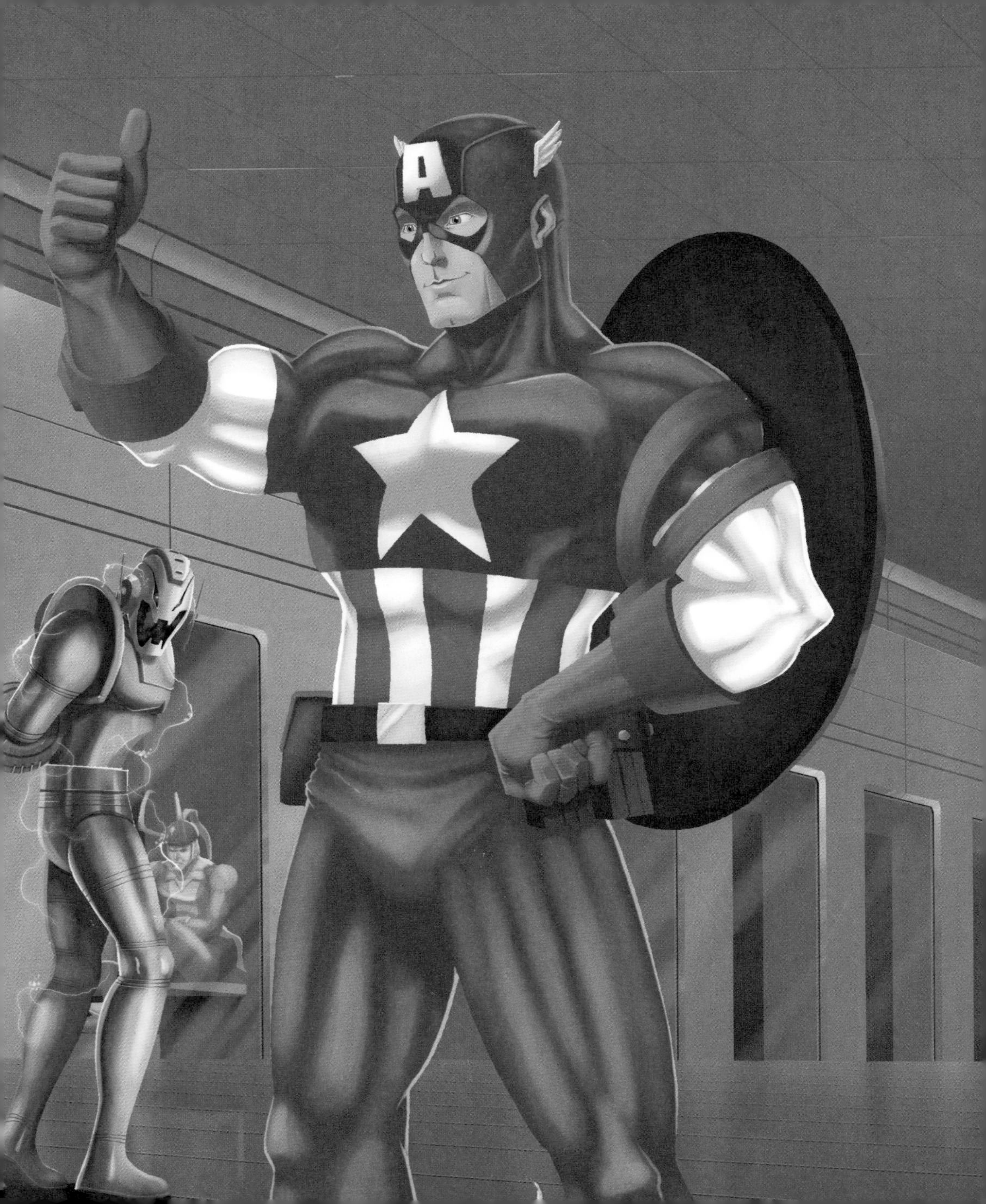

Captain America, Iron Man, Thor, and Hulk are amazing heroes on their own. But as the Avengers, their combined super powers are an unstoppable force for good!

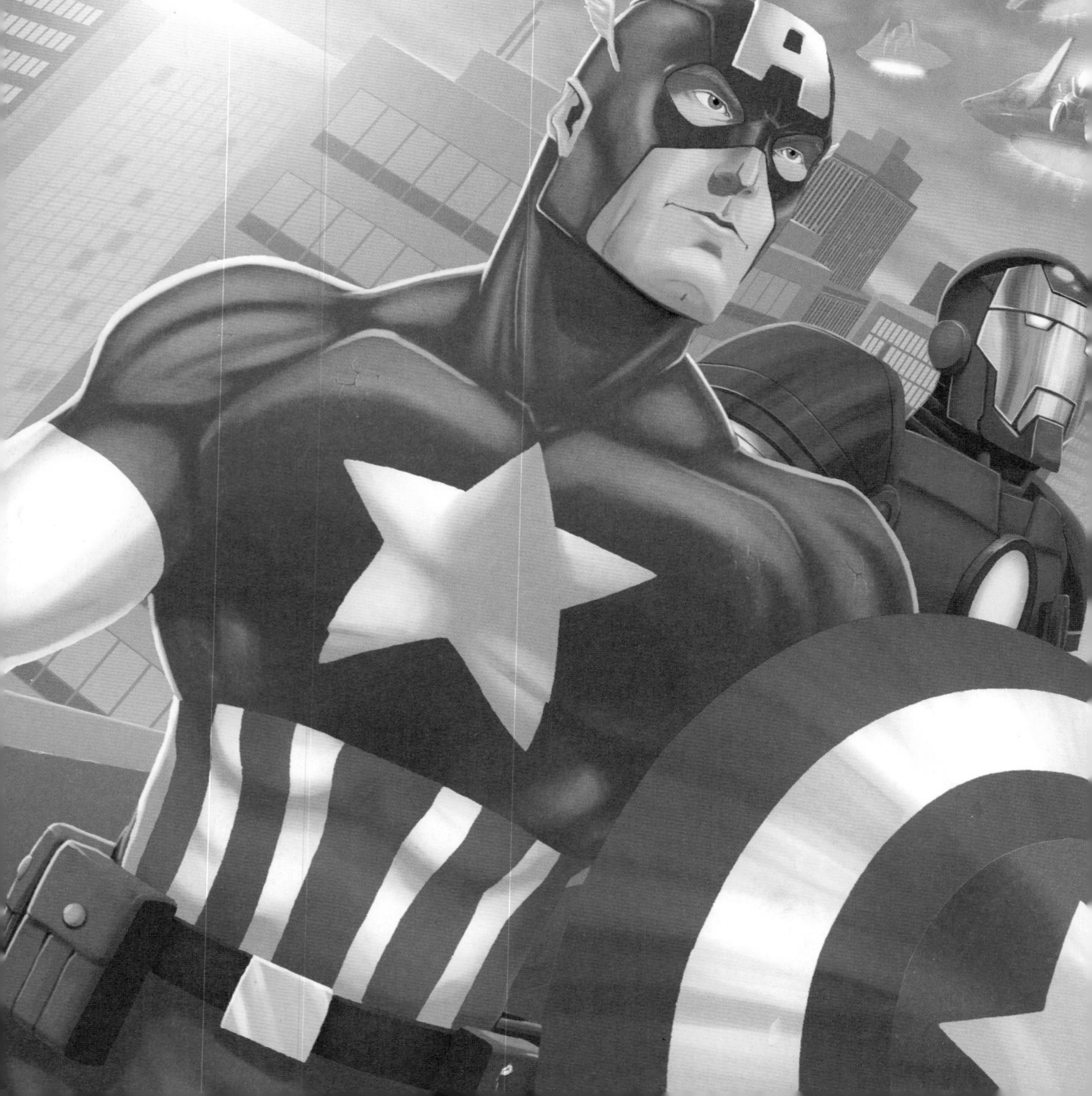

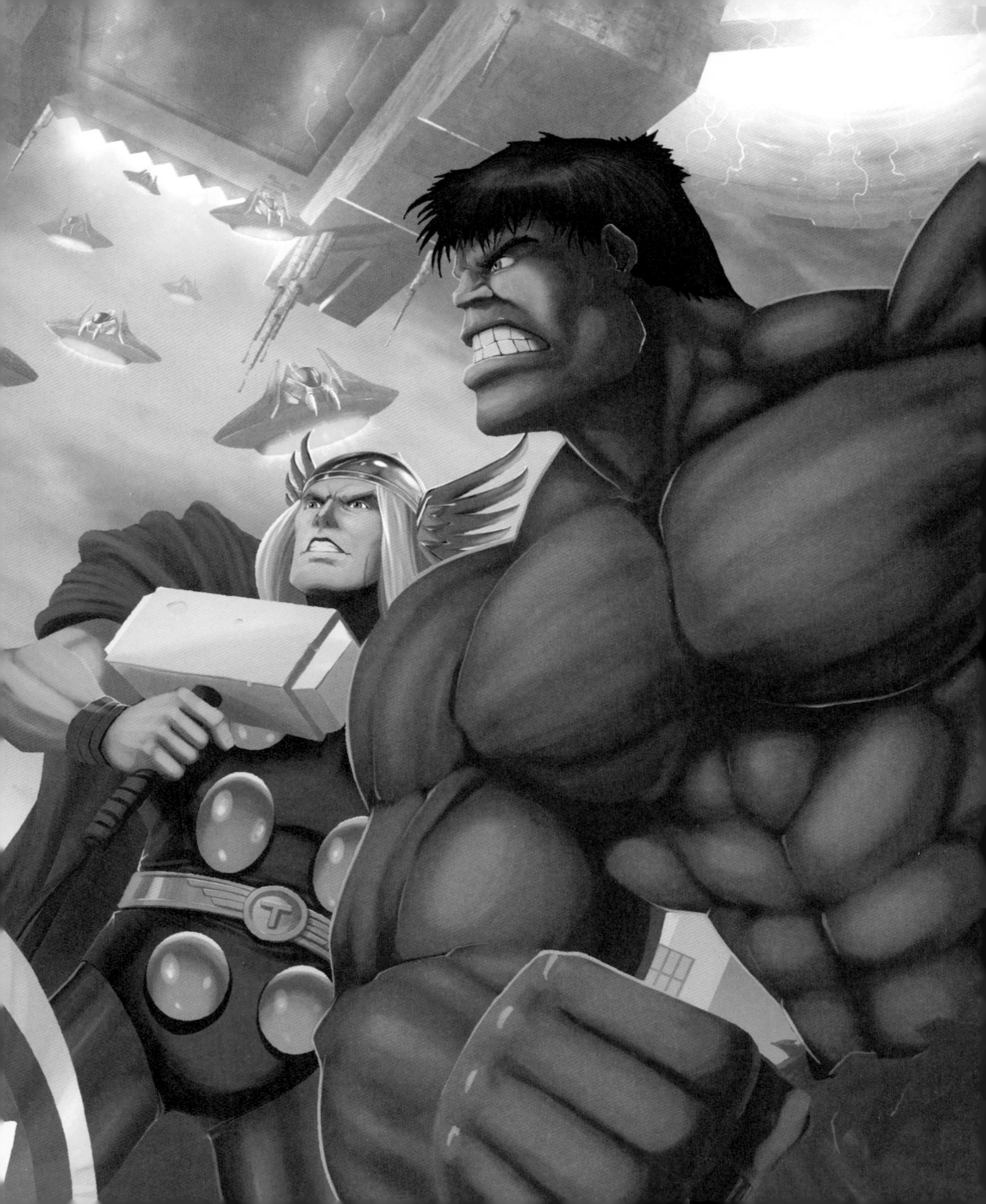

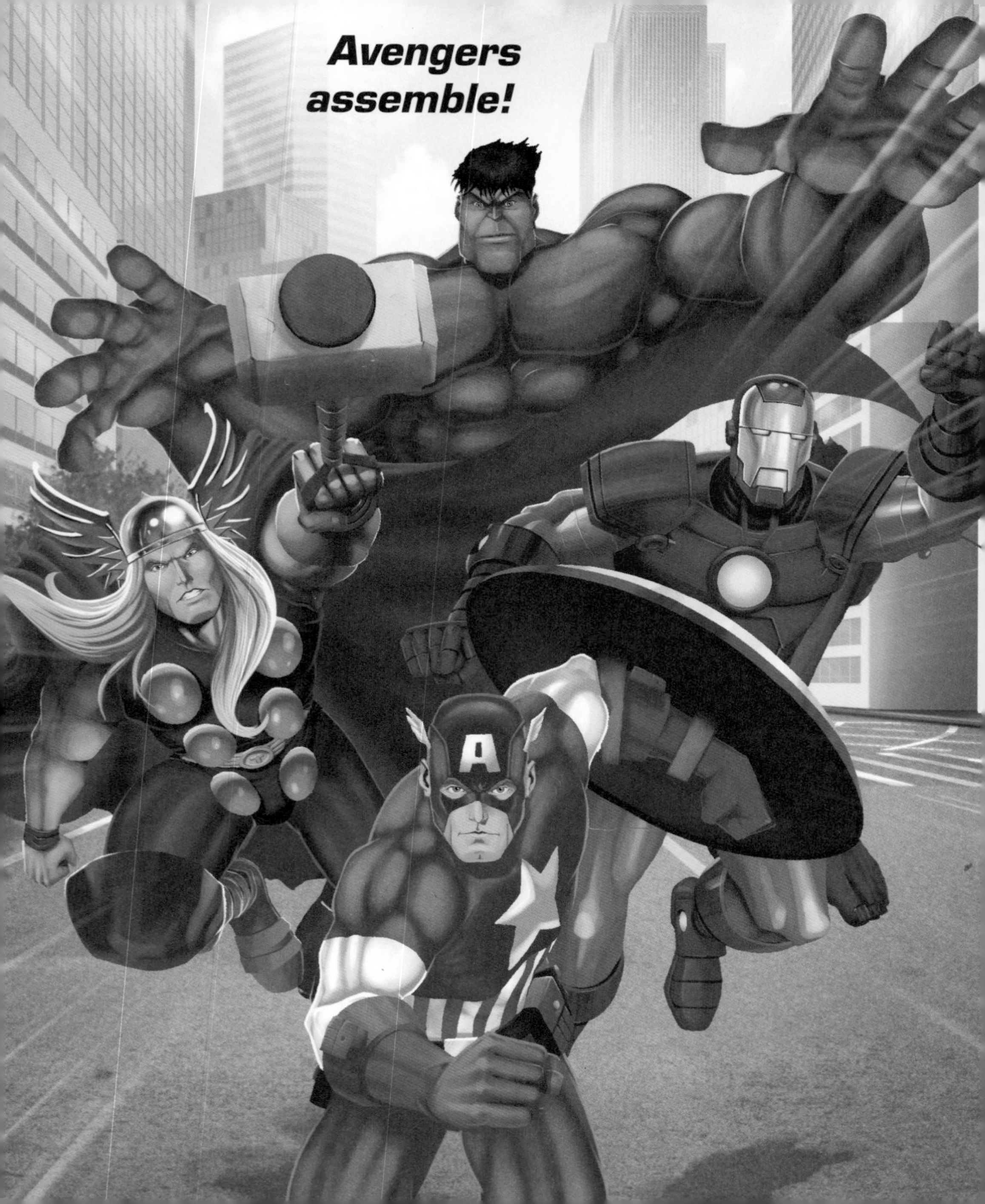
Avengers
assemble!

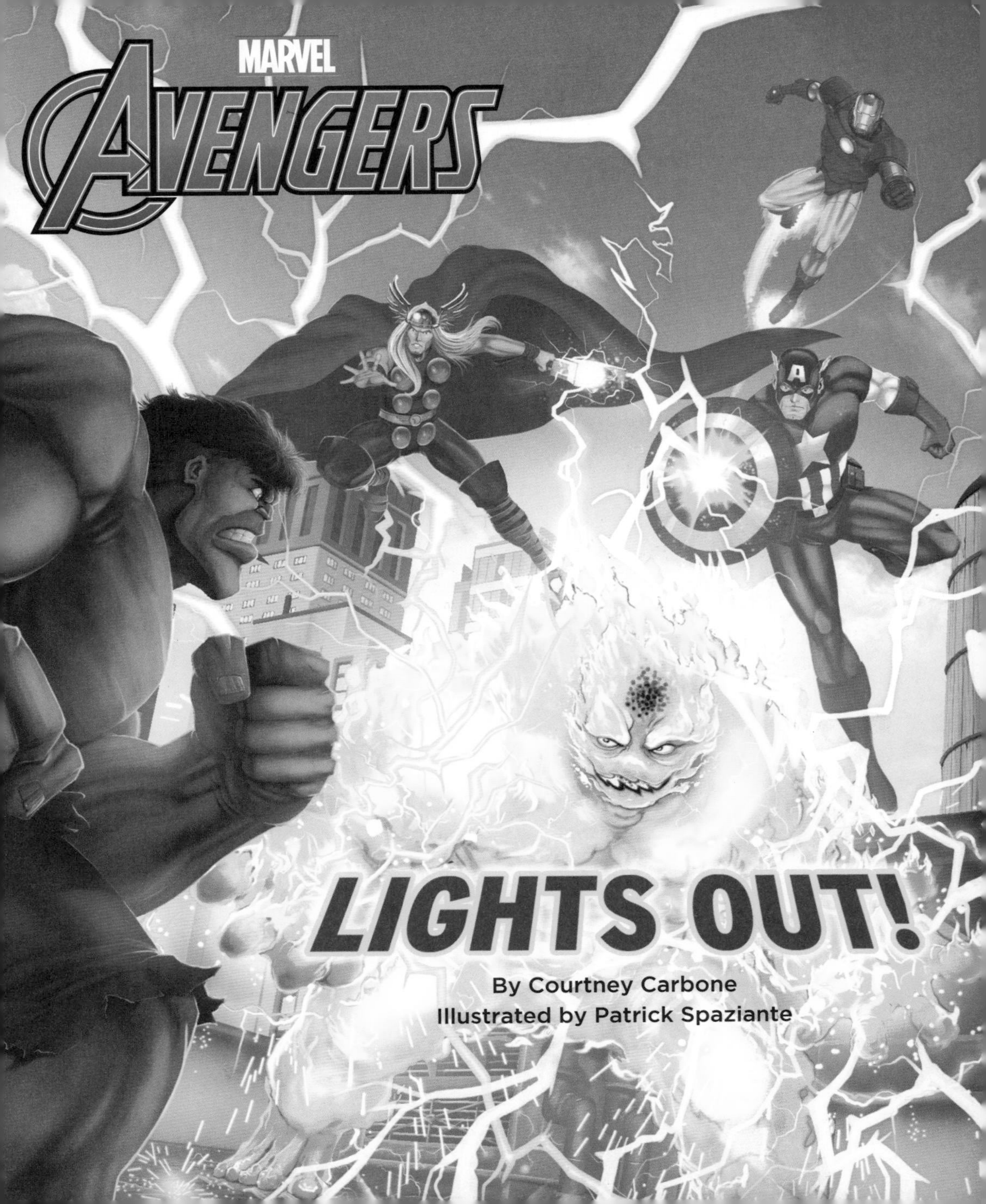

MARVEL AVENGERS

LIGHTS OUT!

By Courtney Carbone
Illustrated by Patrick Spaziante

Iron Man was the leader of the Avengers, a team of super heroes. He loved inventing new devices. His latest creation was a generator that would provide clean power for all of New York City.

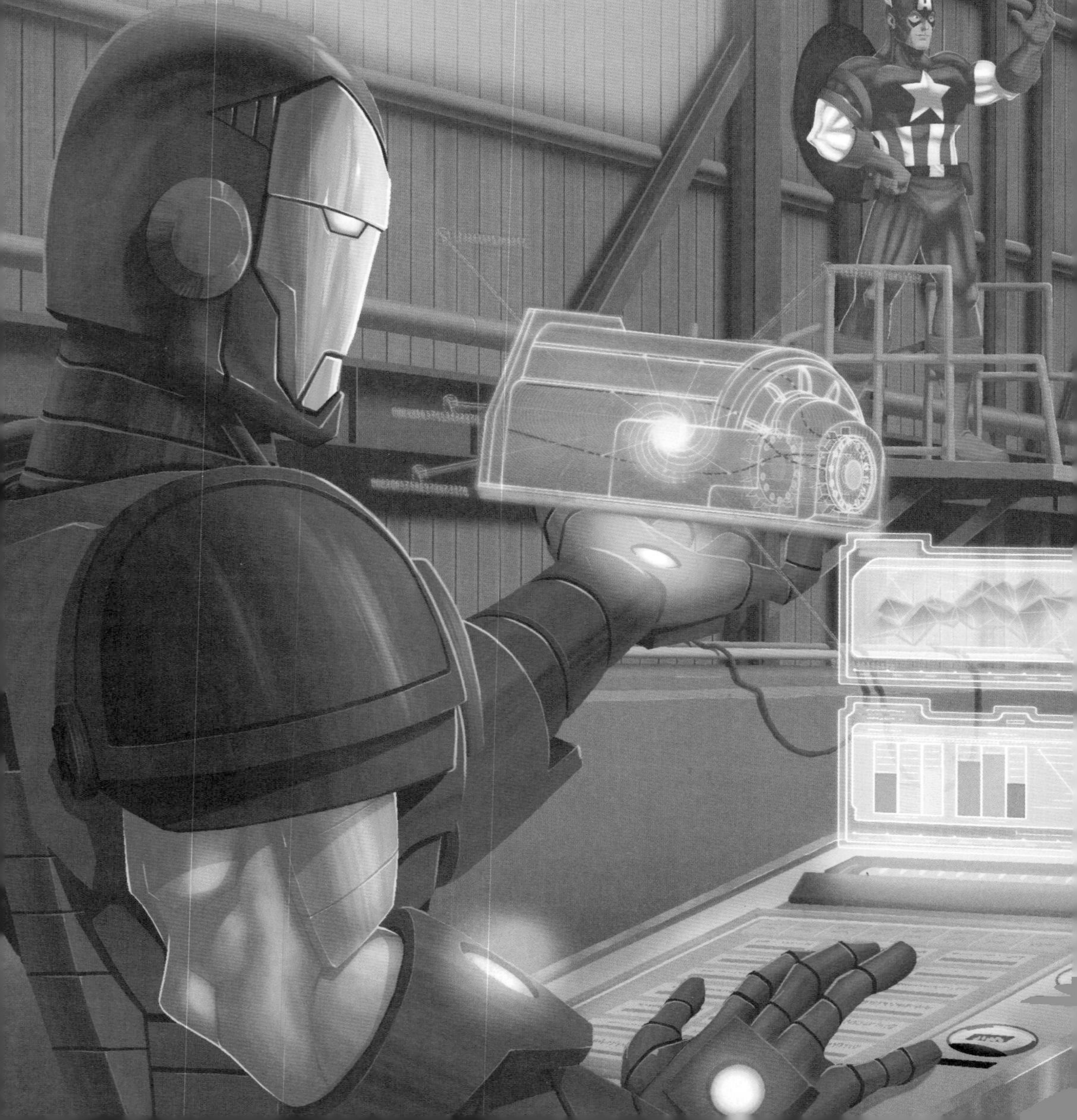

Captain America, Thor, and the Incredible Hulk were helping him install the new generator.

"Careful!" said Iron Man. "It has one hundred times the power of the old generator."

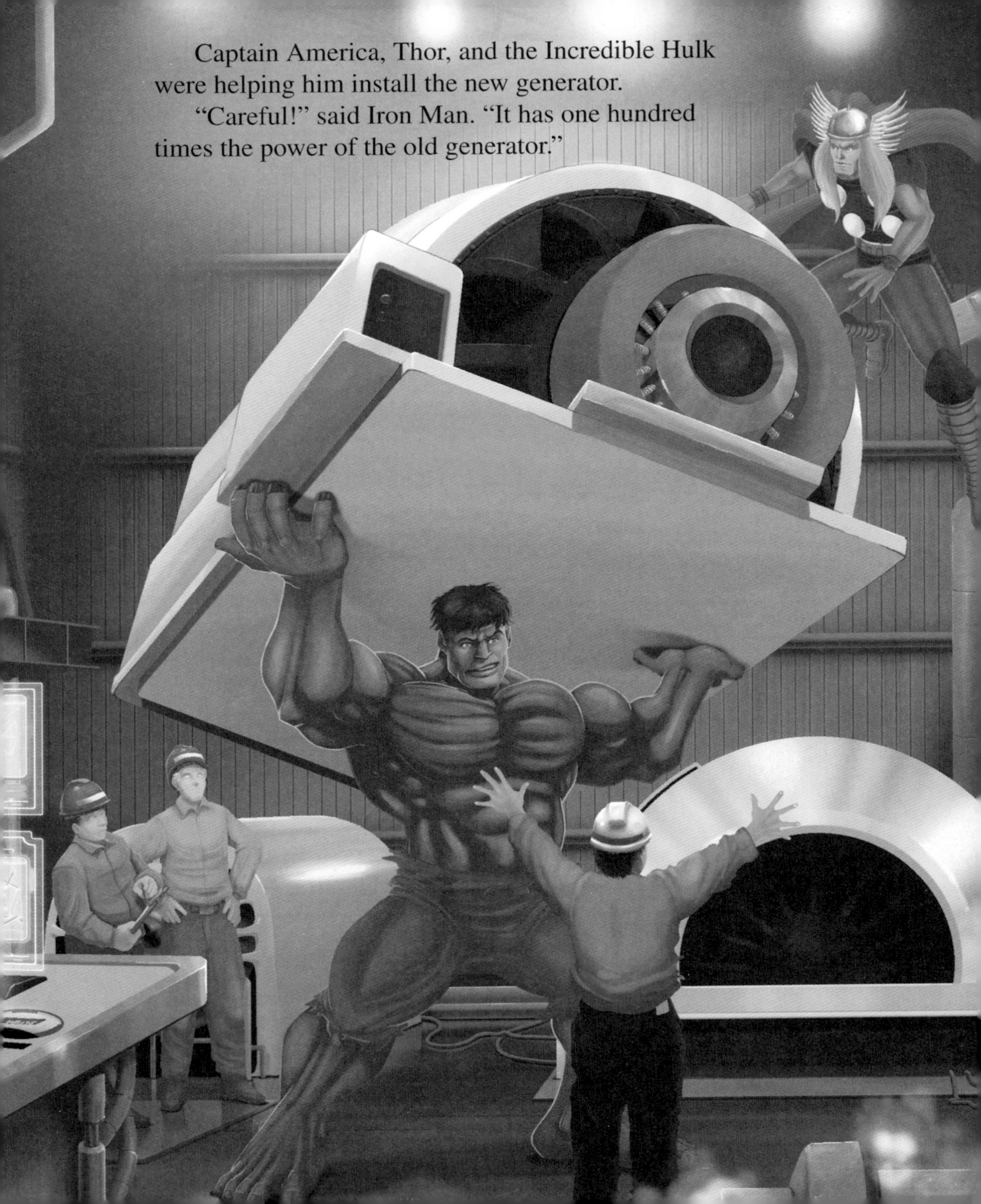

“Wait!” Iron Man shouted. “There are some strange energy readings coming from outside the generator’s system!”

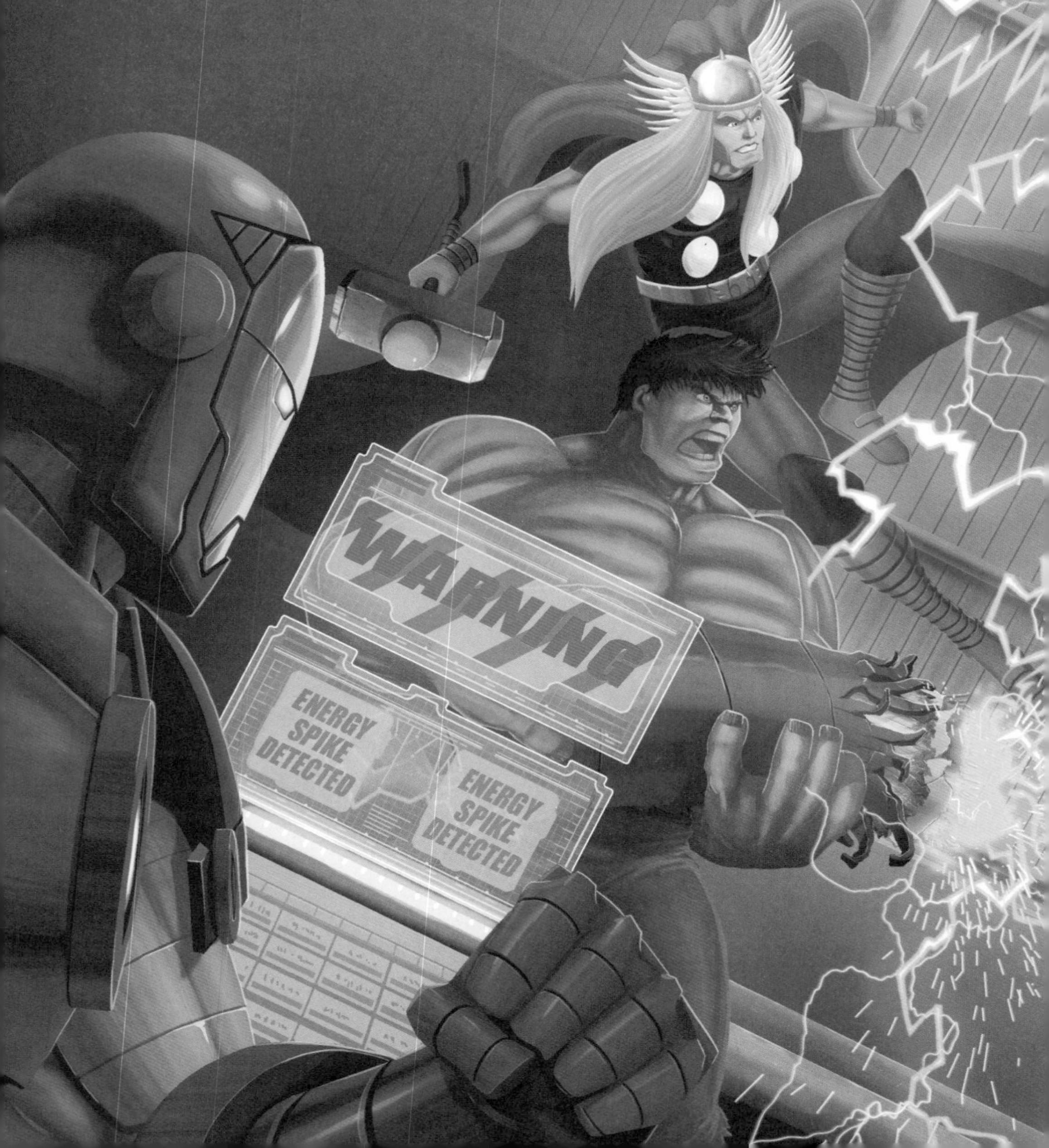
WARNING
ENERGY SPIKE DETECTED
ENERGY SPIKE DETECTED

But it was too late: **BOOM!** The generator exploded! The energy crackled and took on the form of a giant glowing monster.

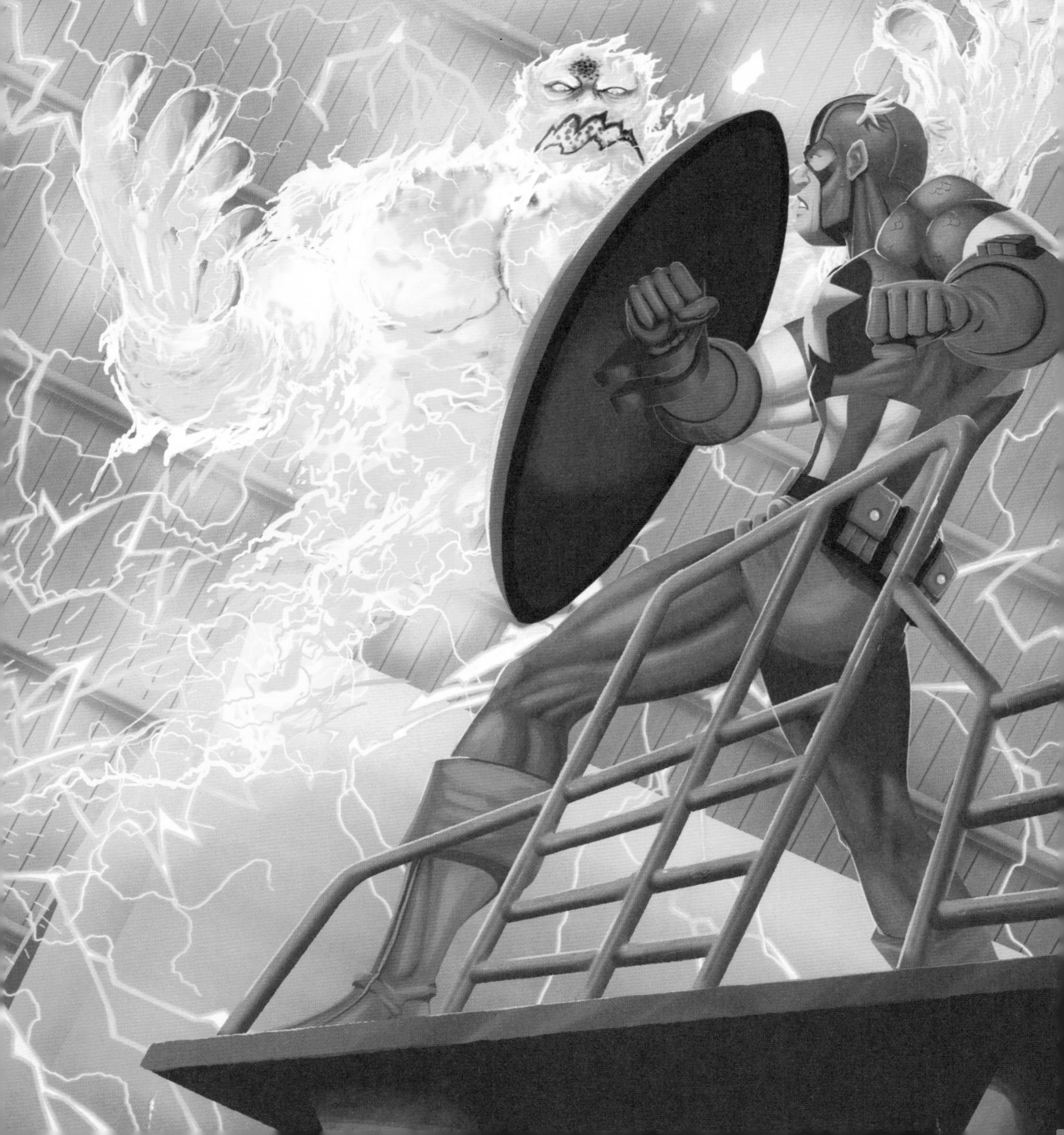

"**Zzzax** lives again!" the creature roared. "Zzzax hungers for more power!"

"Energy monster is Hulk's enemy," Hulk growled. "Hulk SMASH!"

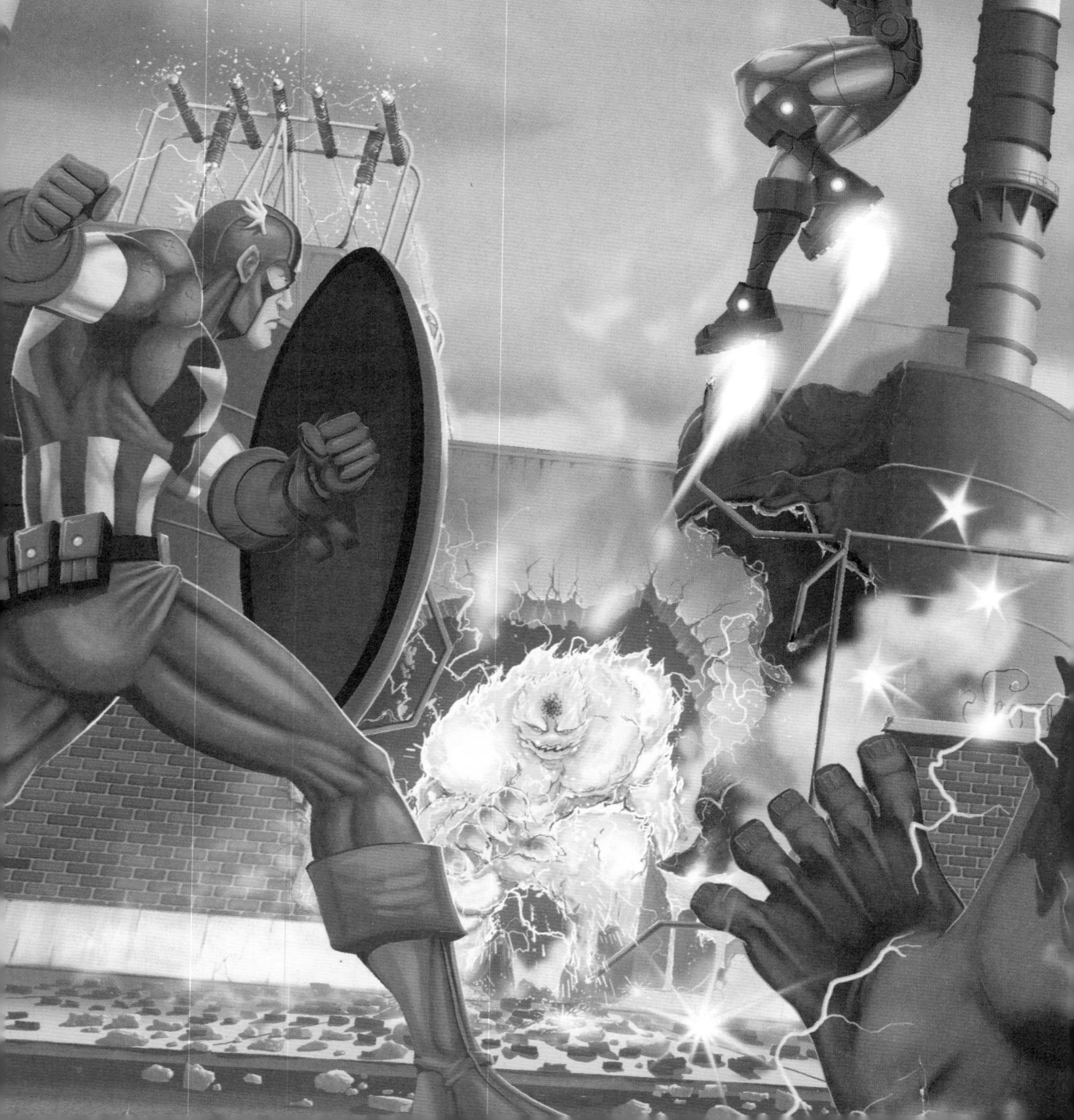

Zzzax unleashed an energy bolt that sent the green giant crashing through a wall.

"City has power!" Zzzax rumbled. He made his way toward the glowing lights of New York.

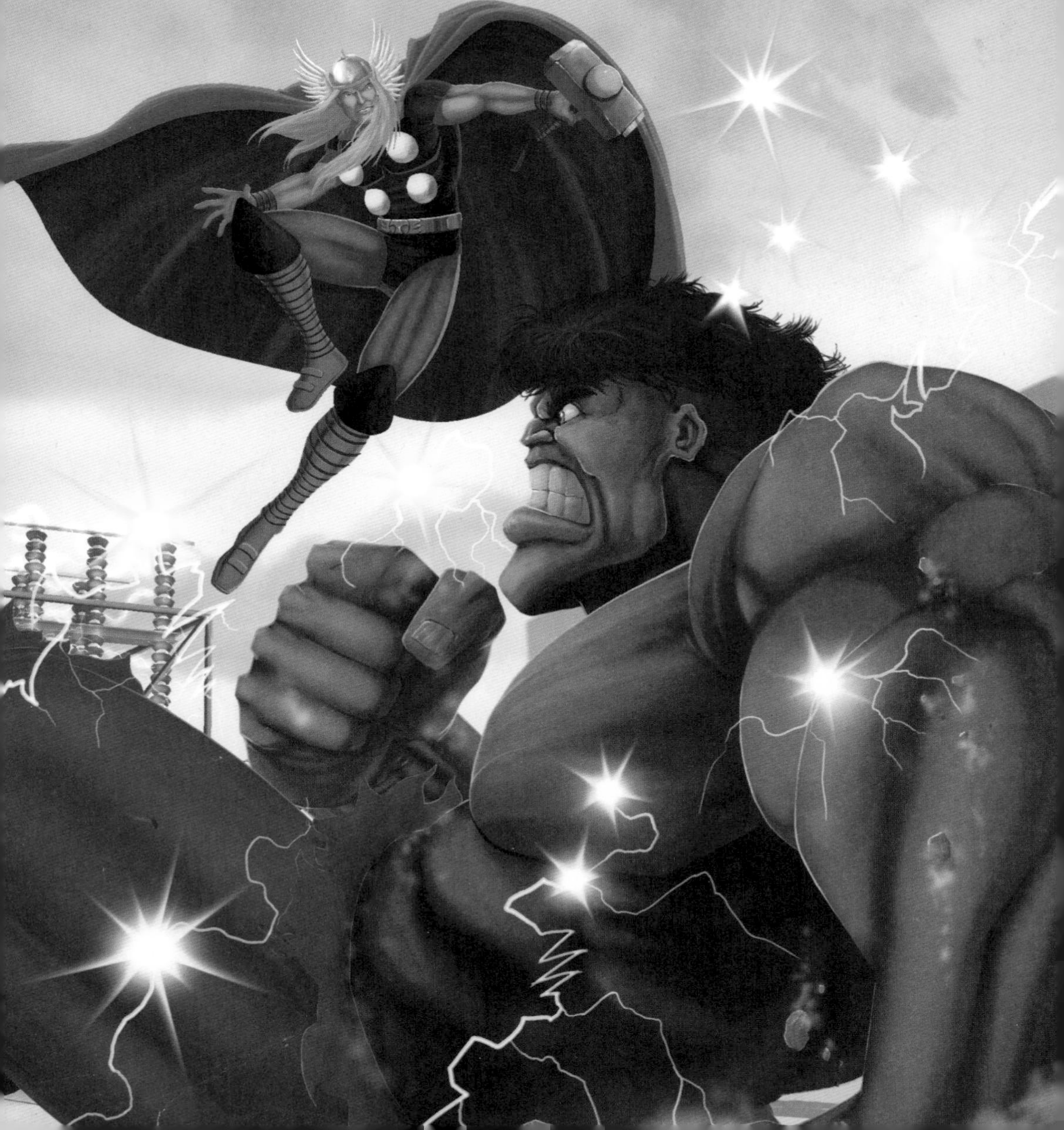

Zzzax stomped into the middle of Times Square. "Power will be mine!" he boomed. Zzzax grew bigger and stronger as he drained energy from the city!

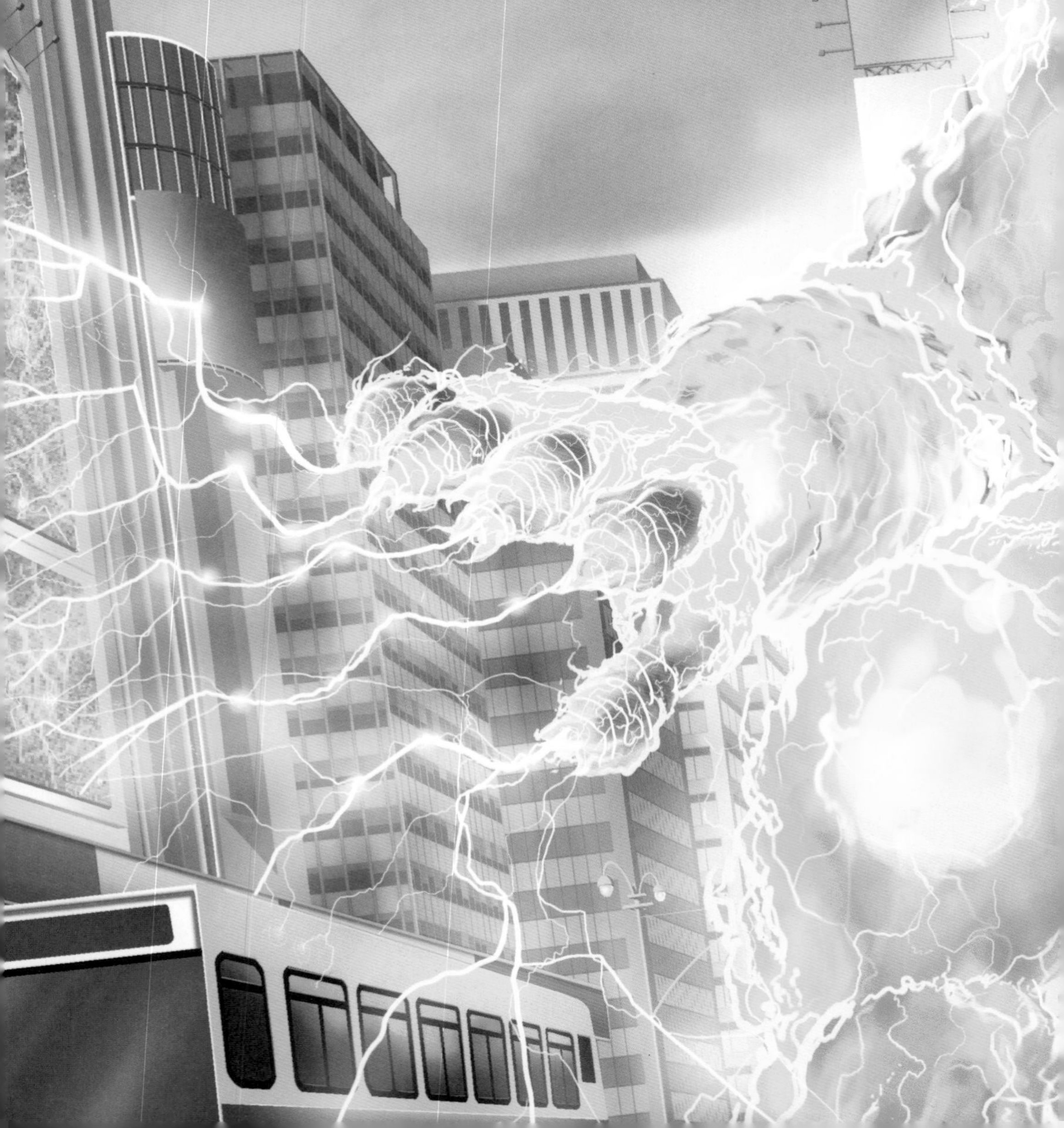

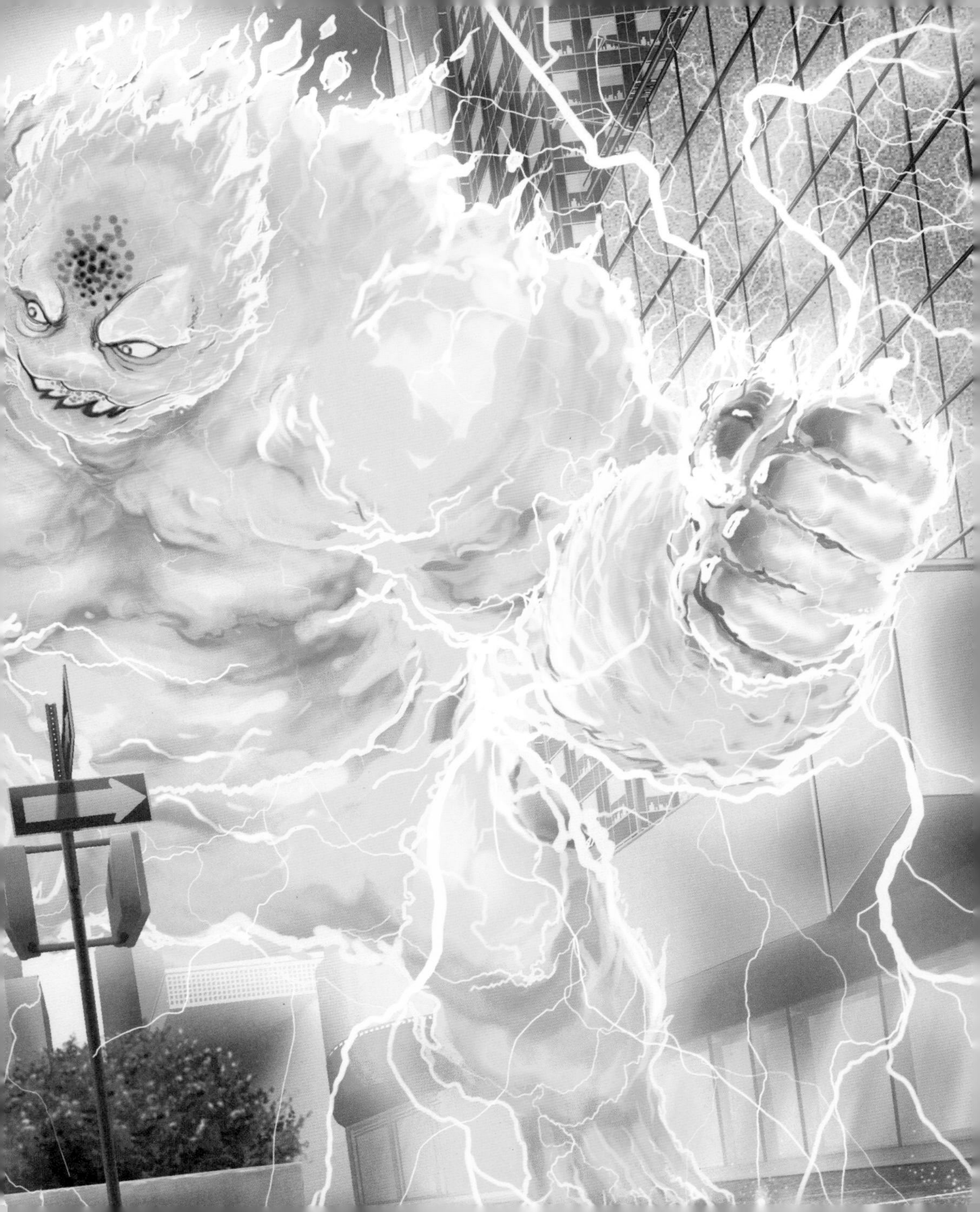

"We have to separate him from his energy source!" Iron Man called to Captain America.

"Distract him, Avengers," Captain America replied, "while I cut off his power with my shield!"

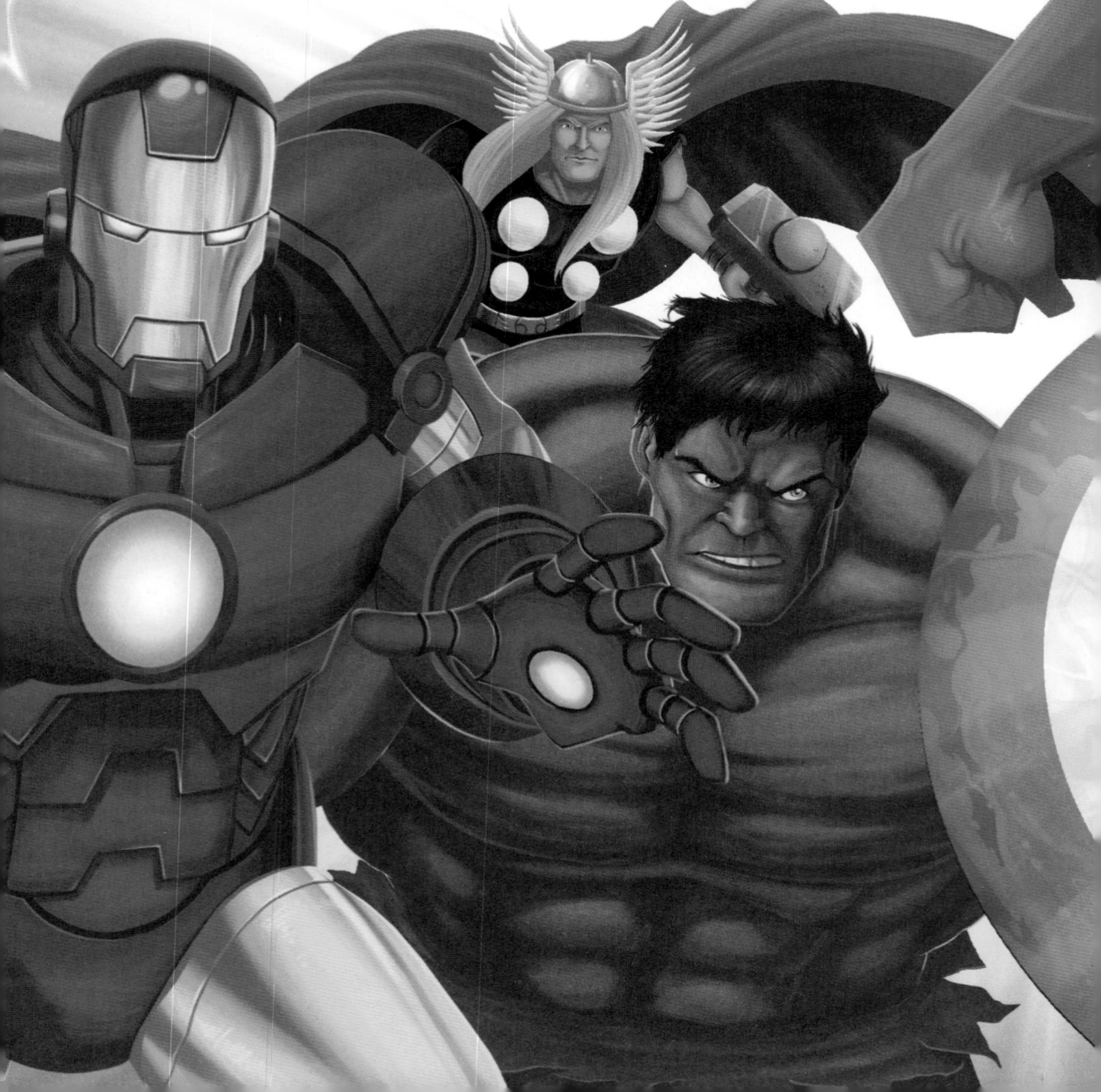

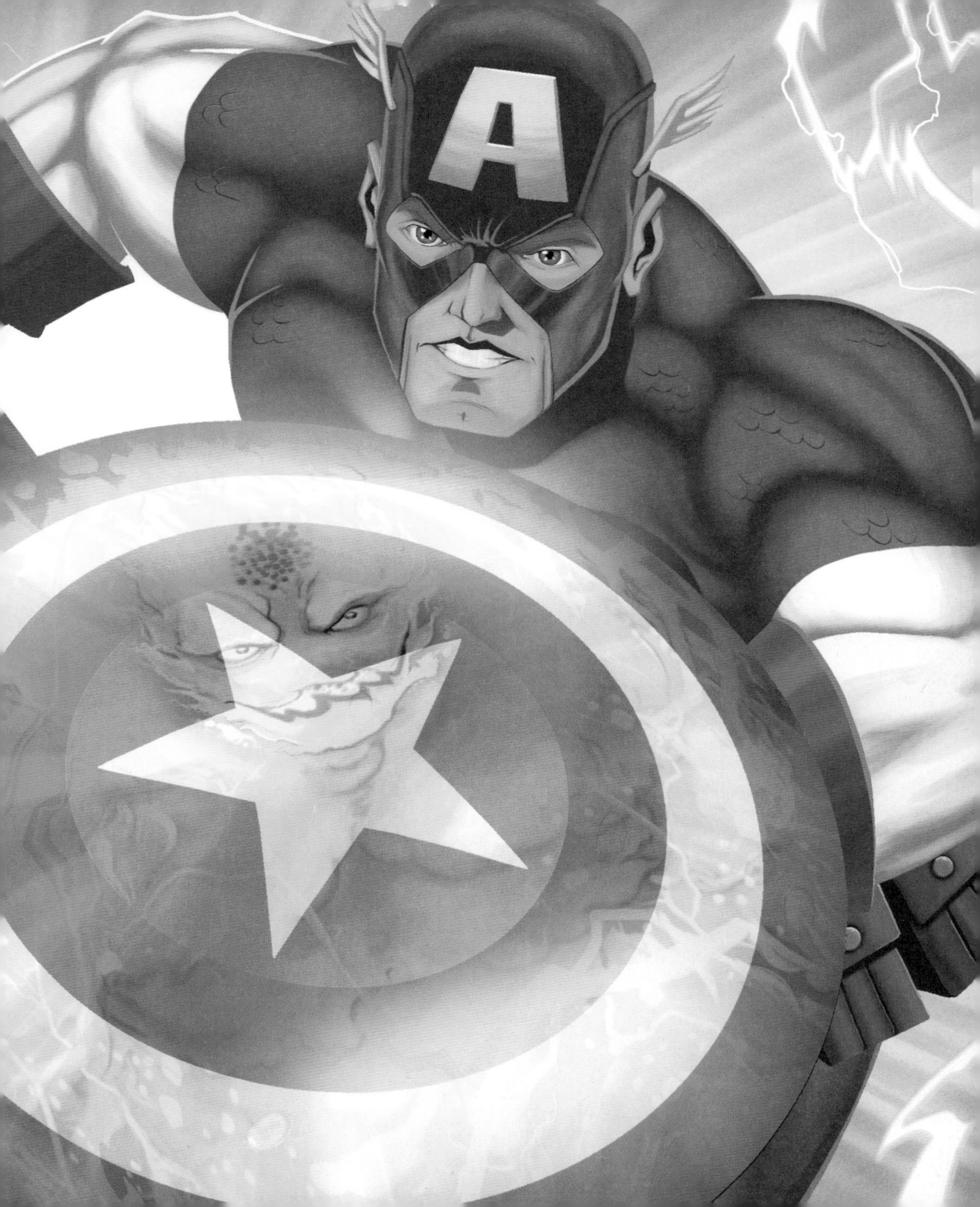

The Avengers attacked Zzzax. The monster swatted at them, but the heroes were too strong and too fast.

"Keep him busy, Avengers!" Iron Man shouted. "Now, Cap!"

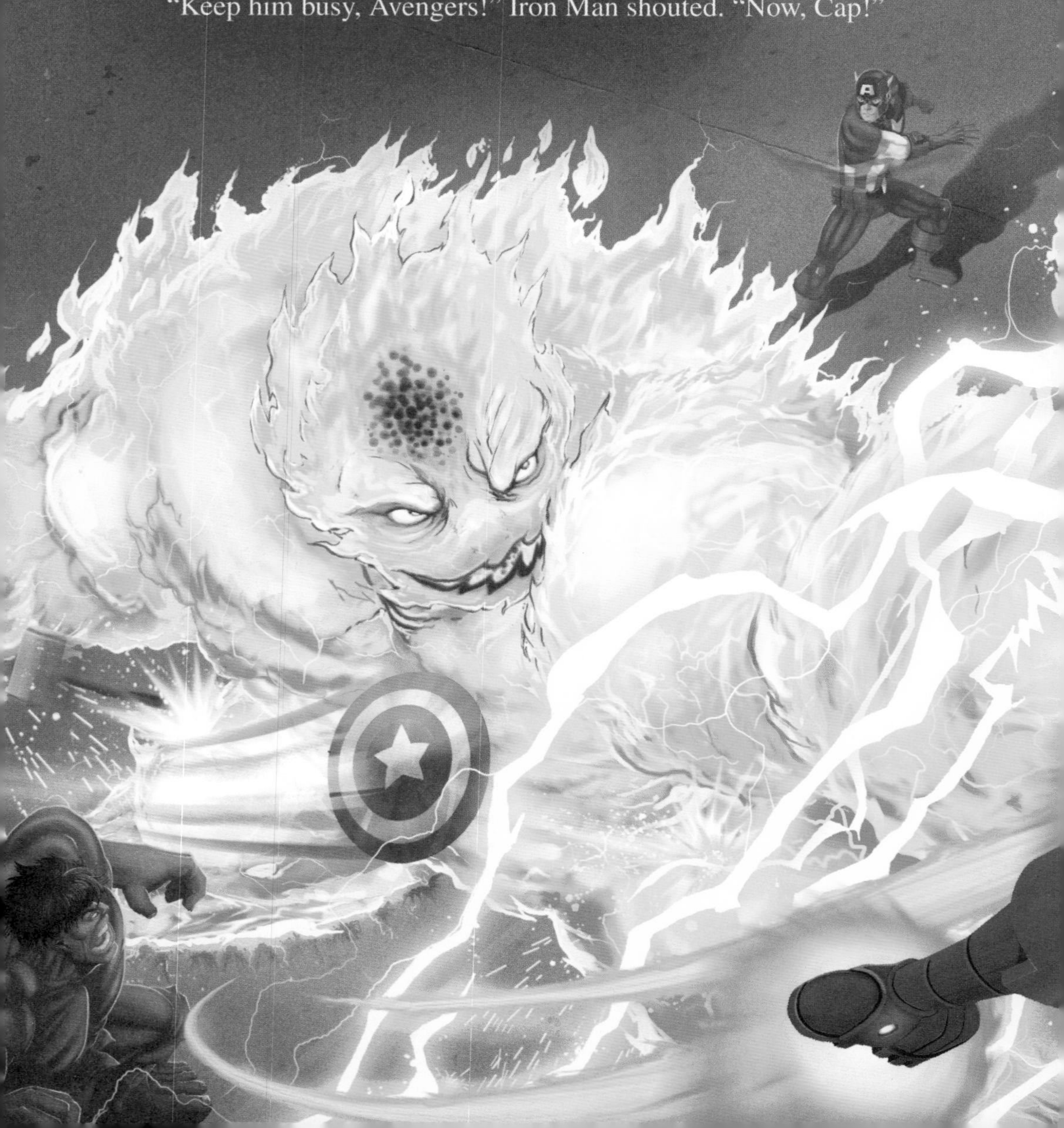

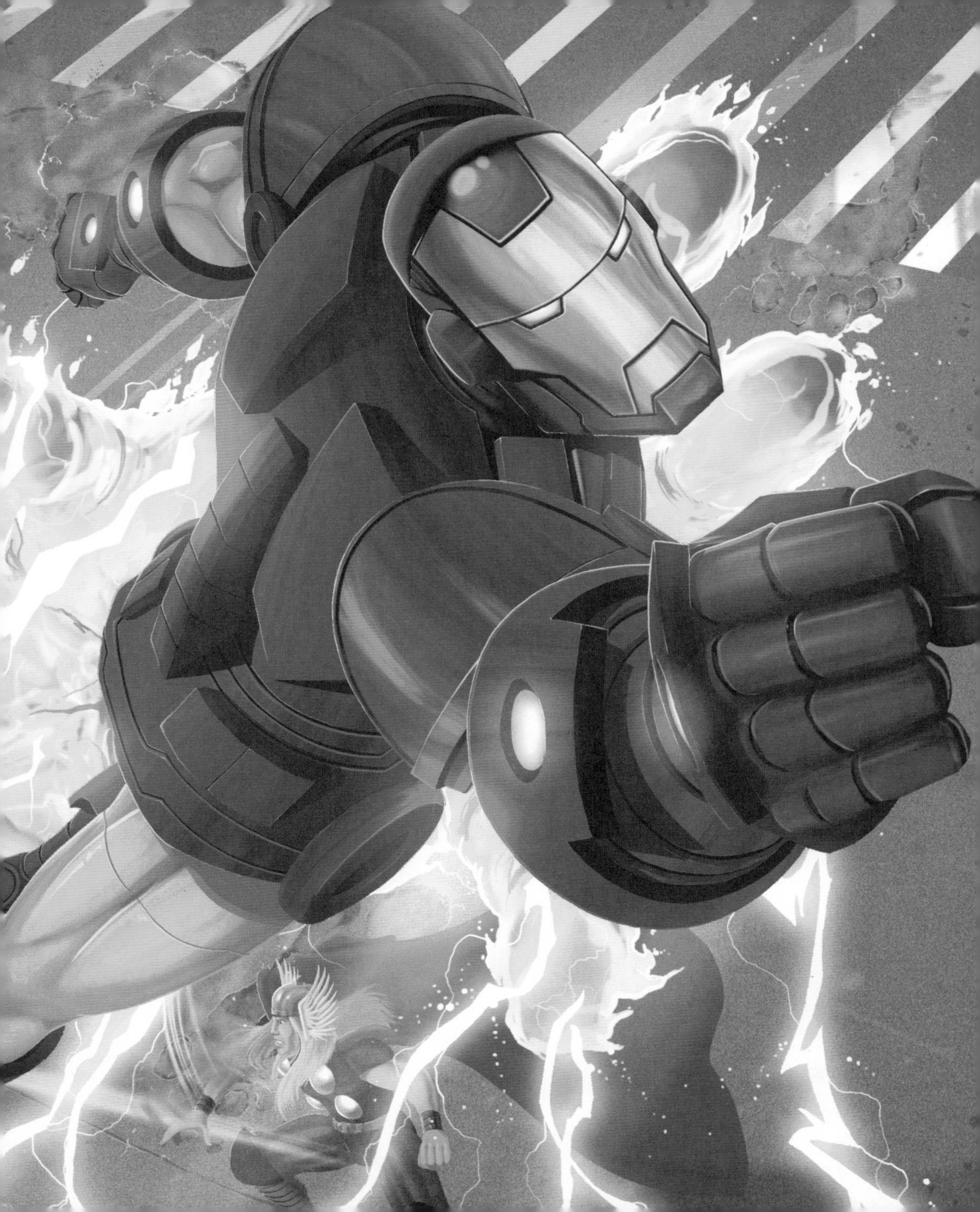

Captain America threw his mighty shield. It sliced through the arcs of electricity, interrupting the flow of power to the monster.

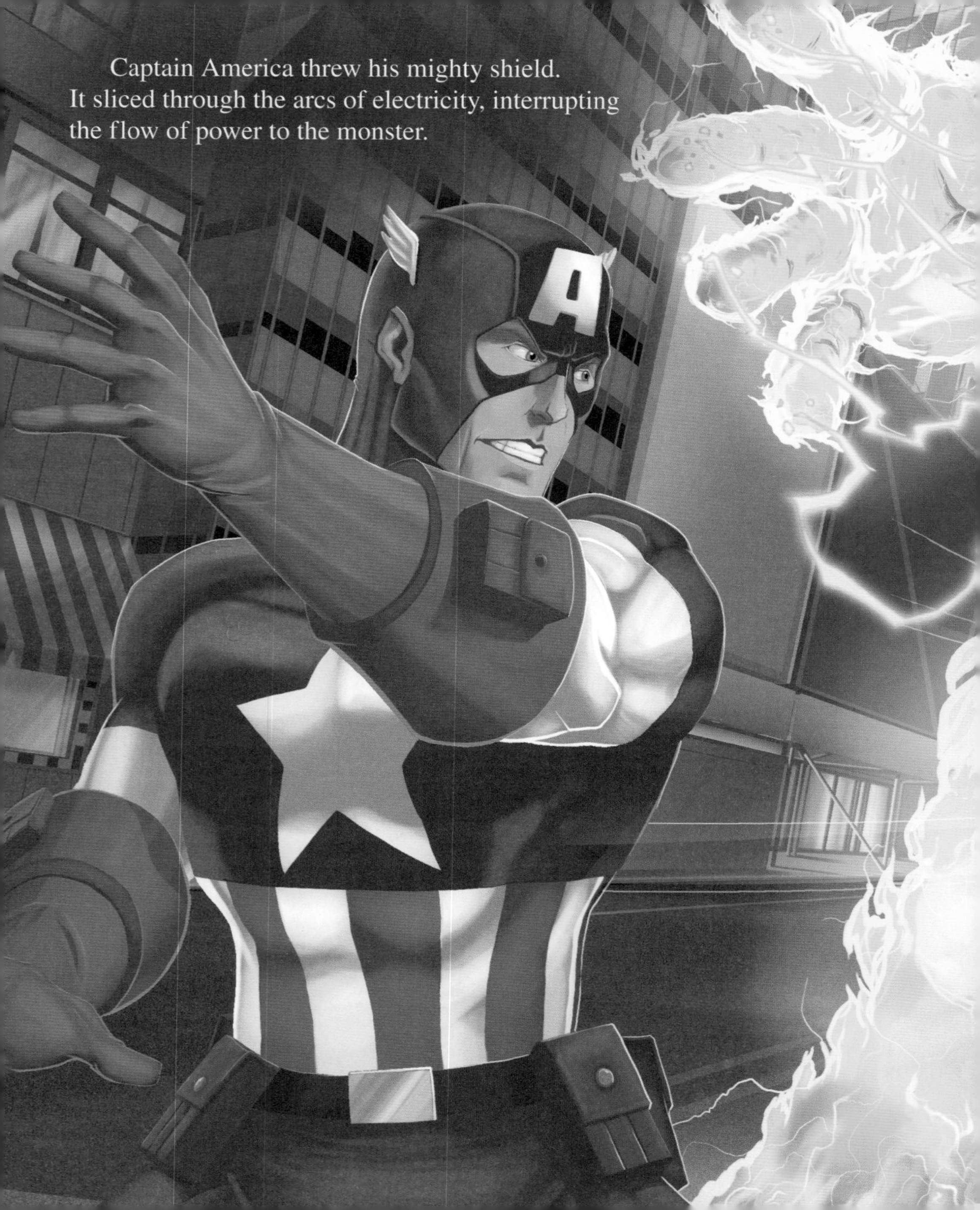

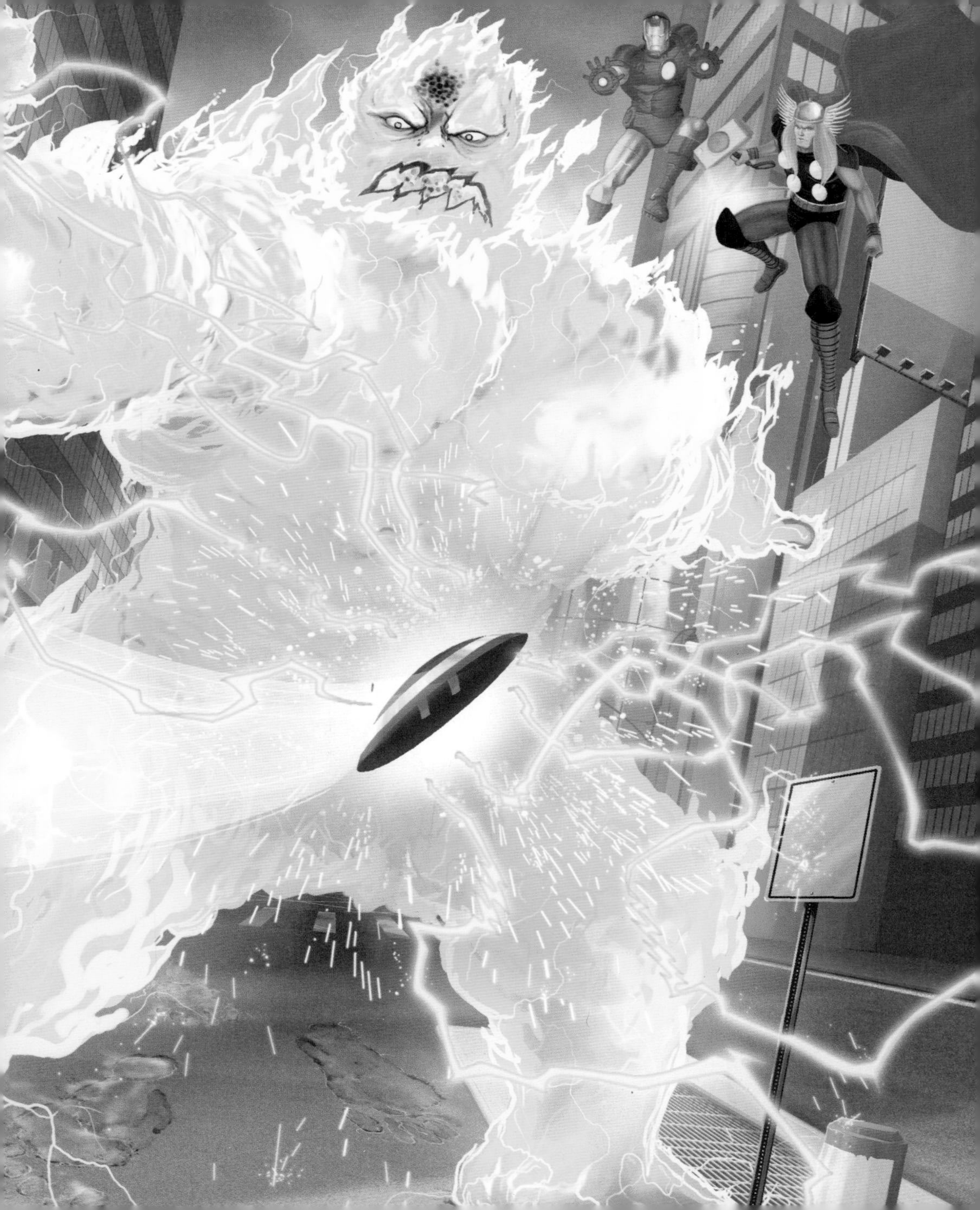

With his power cut off, Zzzax began to get smaller. "Hulk stop Zzzax!" the green giant roared as he cracked open a nearby fire hydrant. "Hulk SPLASH!"

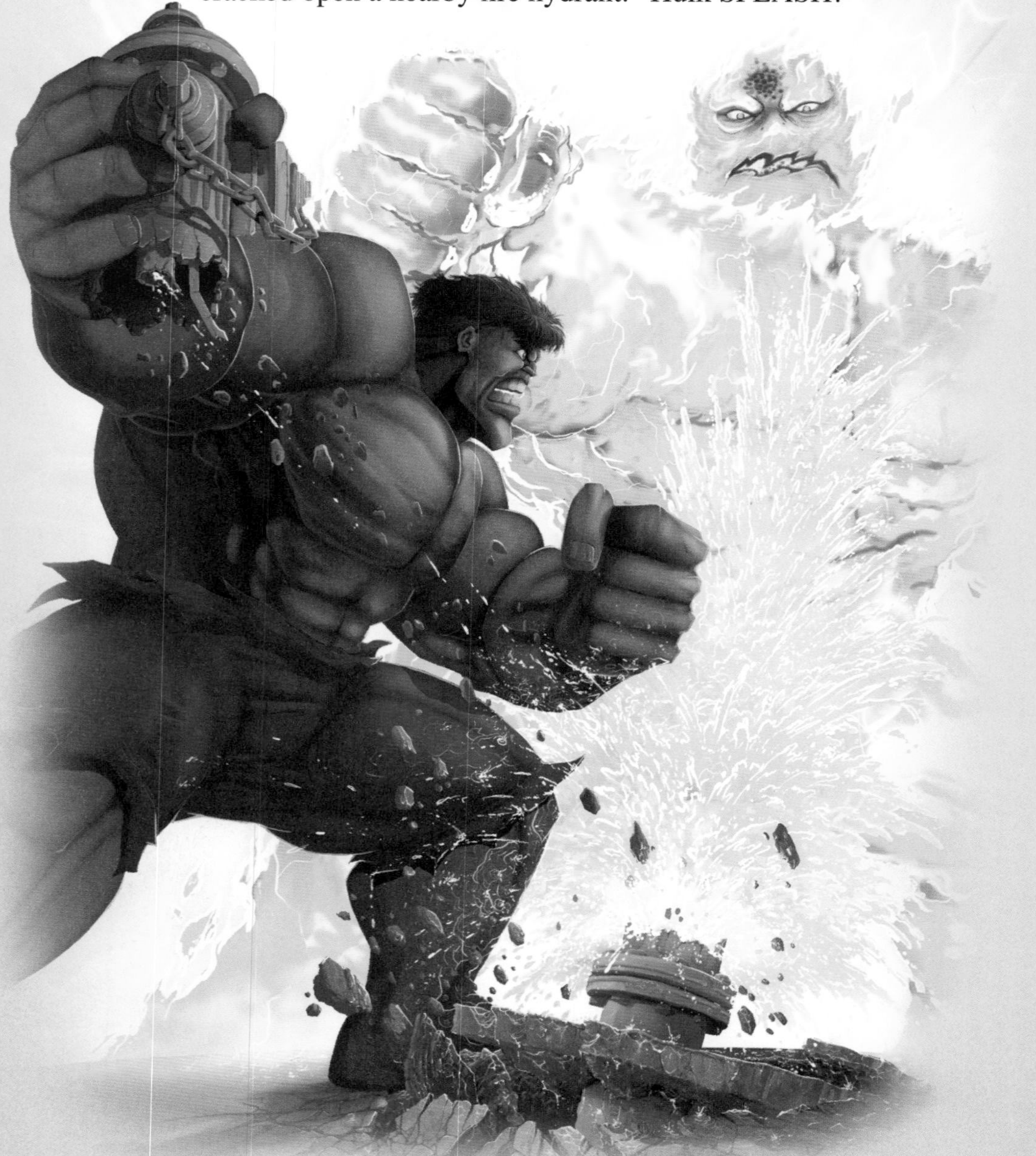

Water from the hydrant hit the monster, causing him to spark and short-circuit. Zzzax's energy began to drain away. "Zzzax is all washed up!" Captain America said.

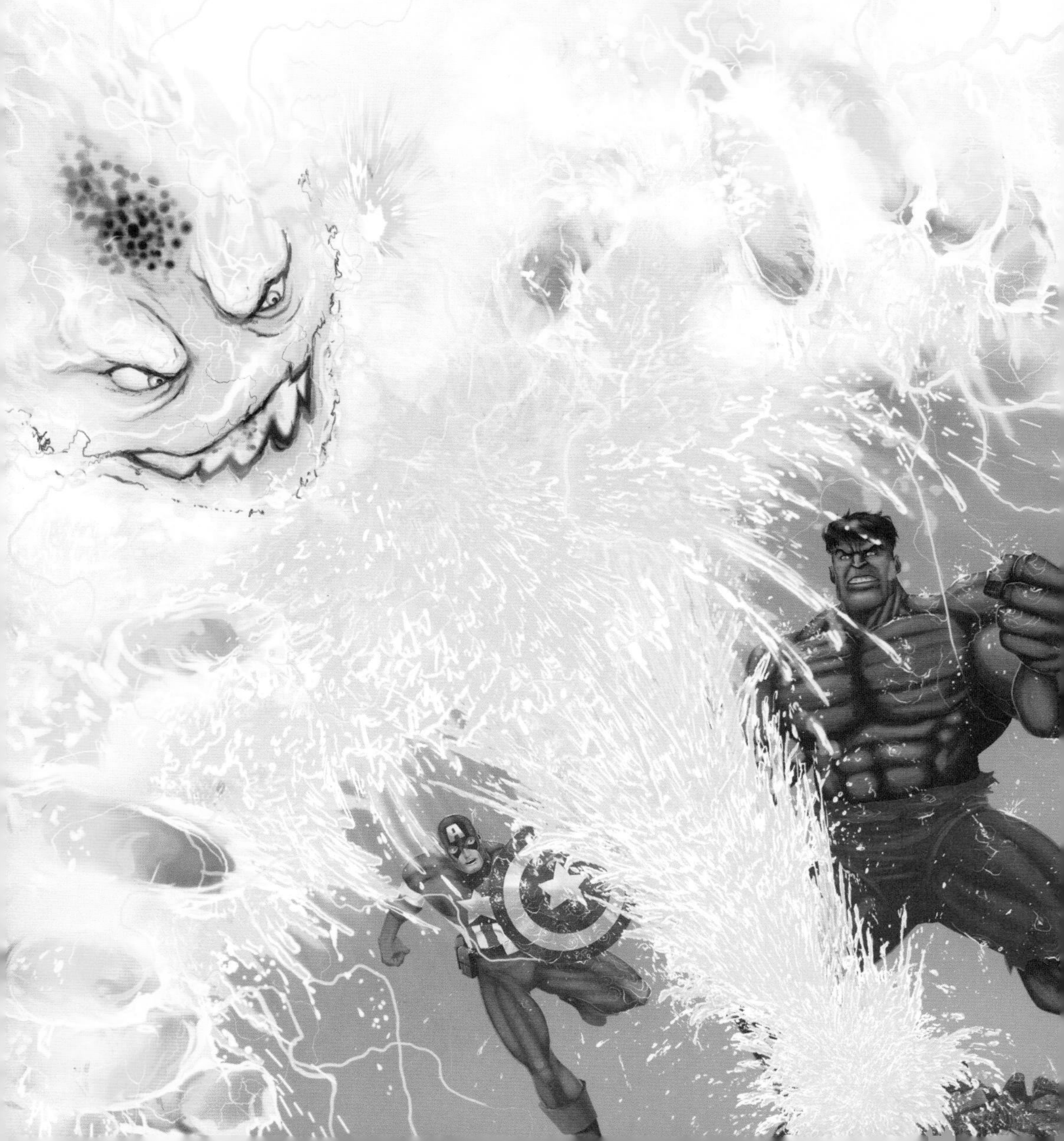

“And now to finish the task!” Thor declared. He used his mighty hammer to soak up Zzzax’s remaining energy.

“Lights out for you, Zzzax!” said Iron Man.

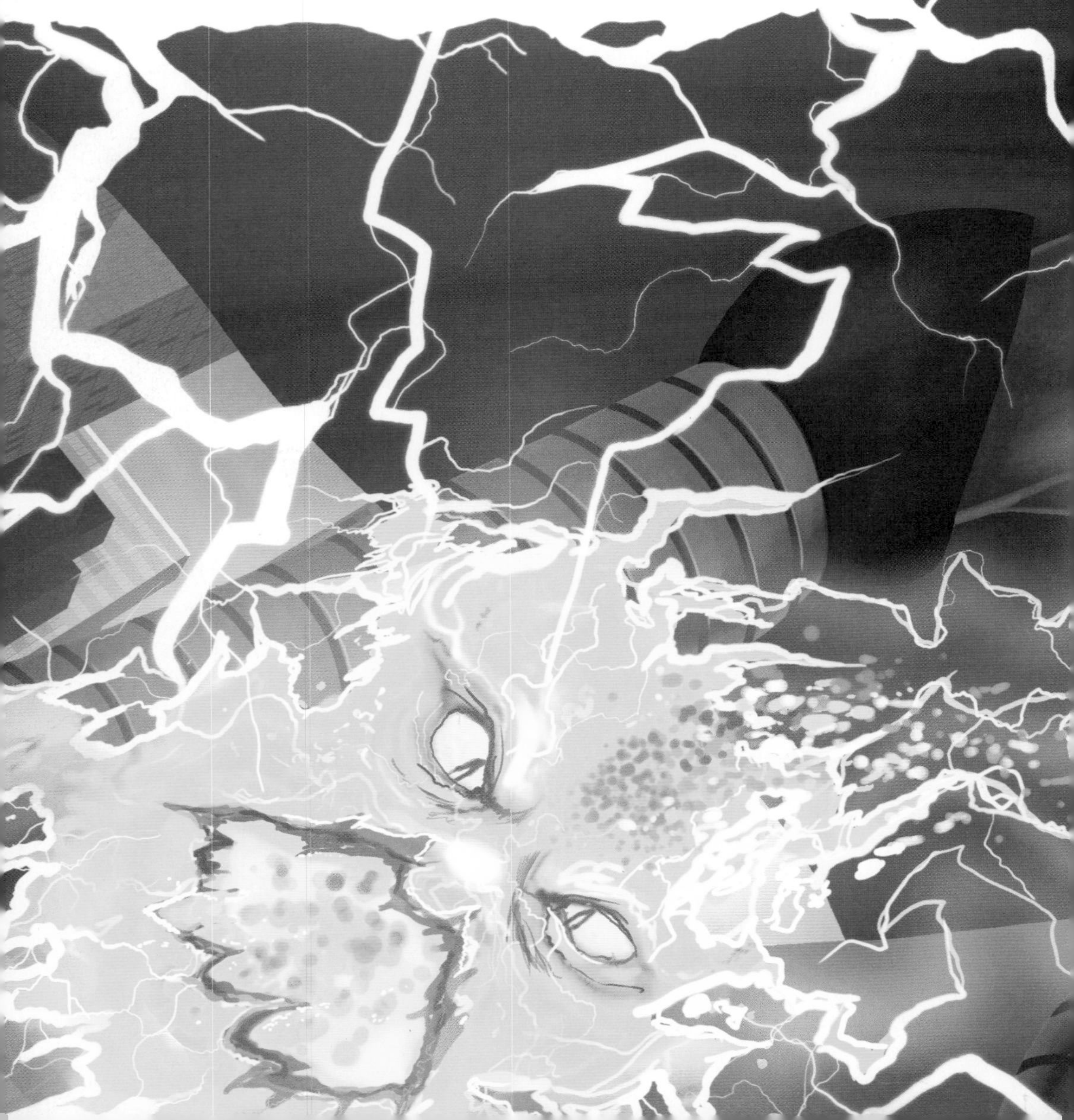

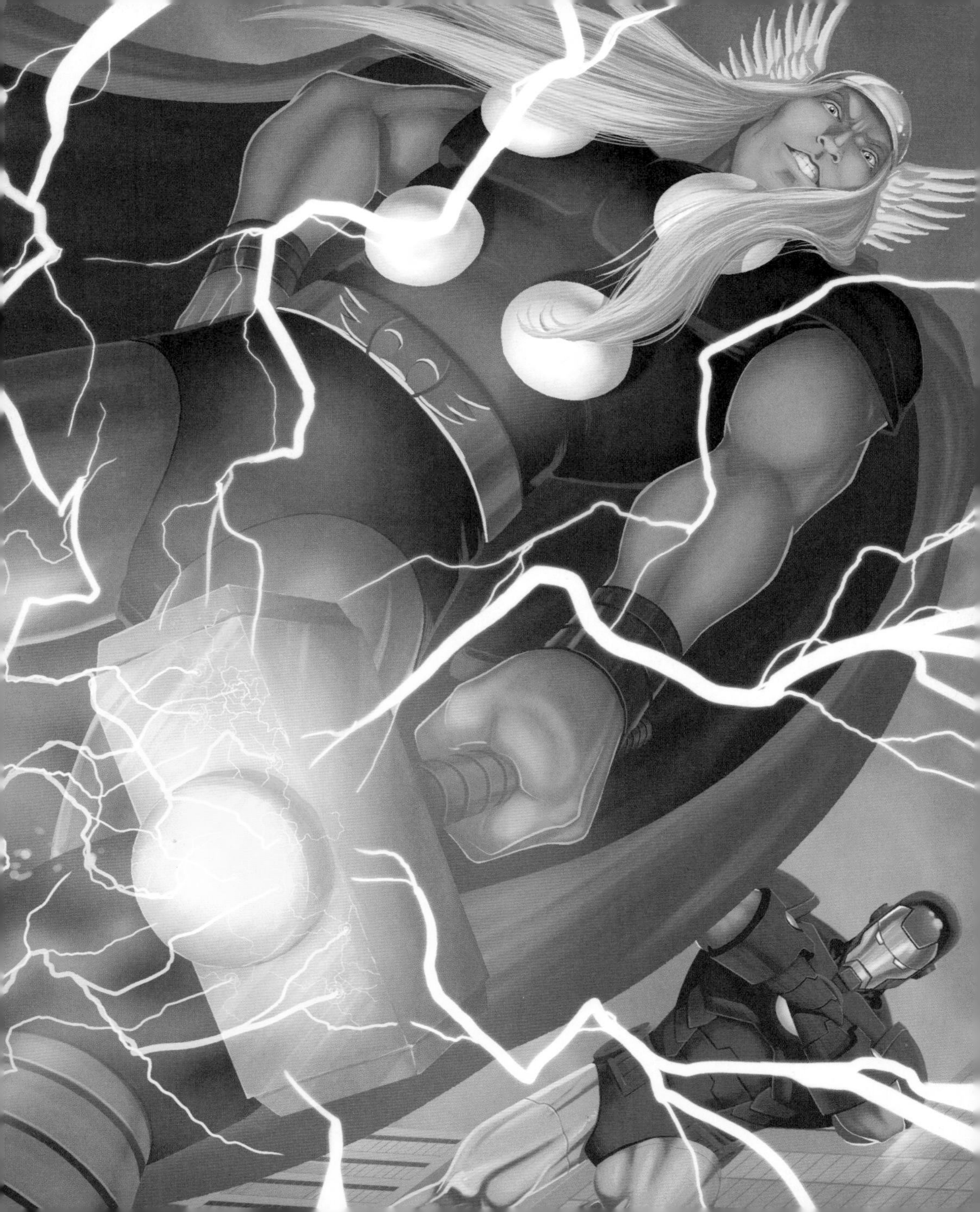

Then Thor held the hammer high above his head.

"Power, back from whence you came!" he thundered, releasing the energy. The city lit up once more!

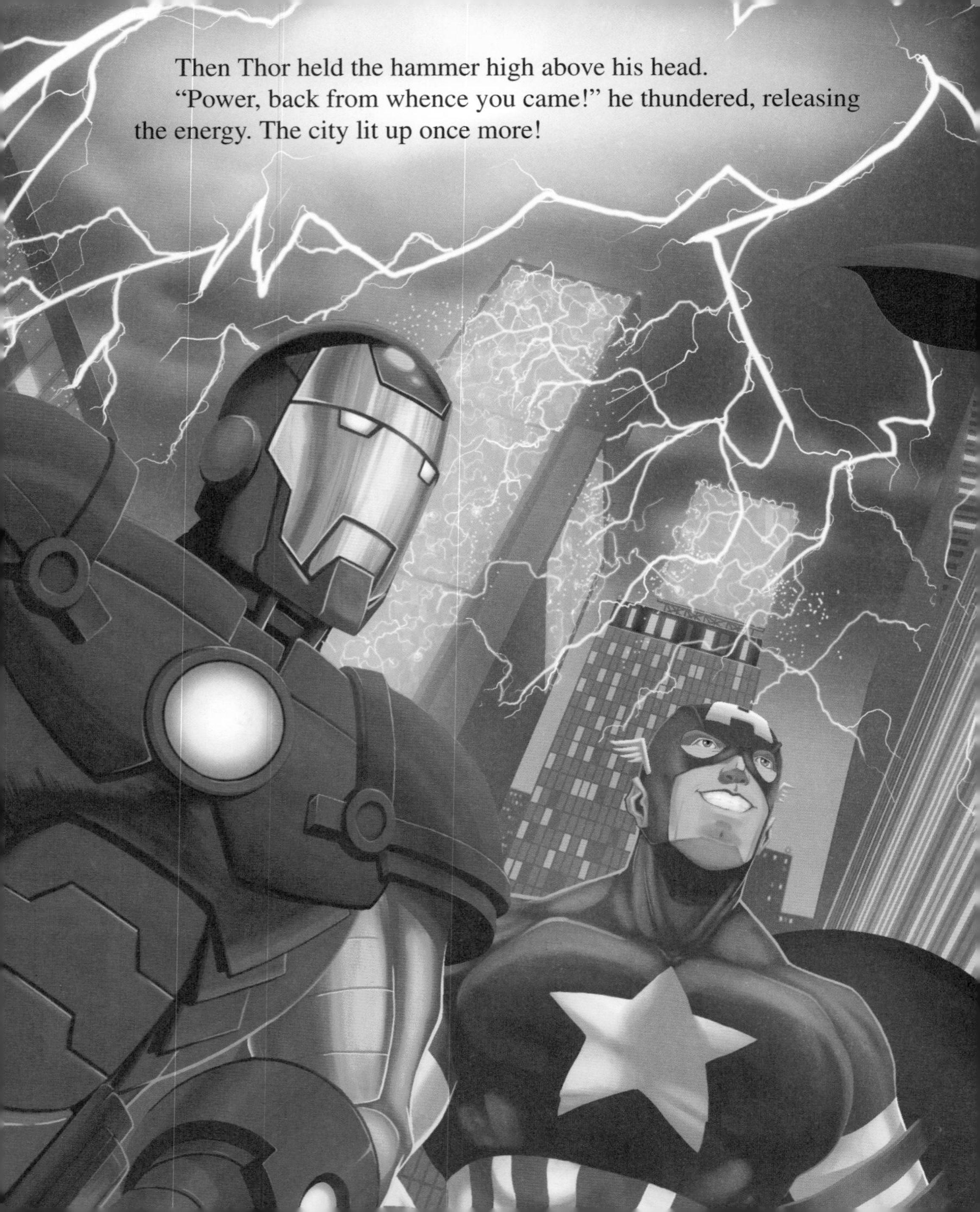

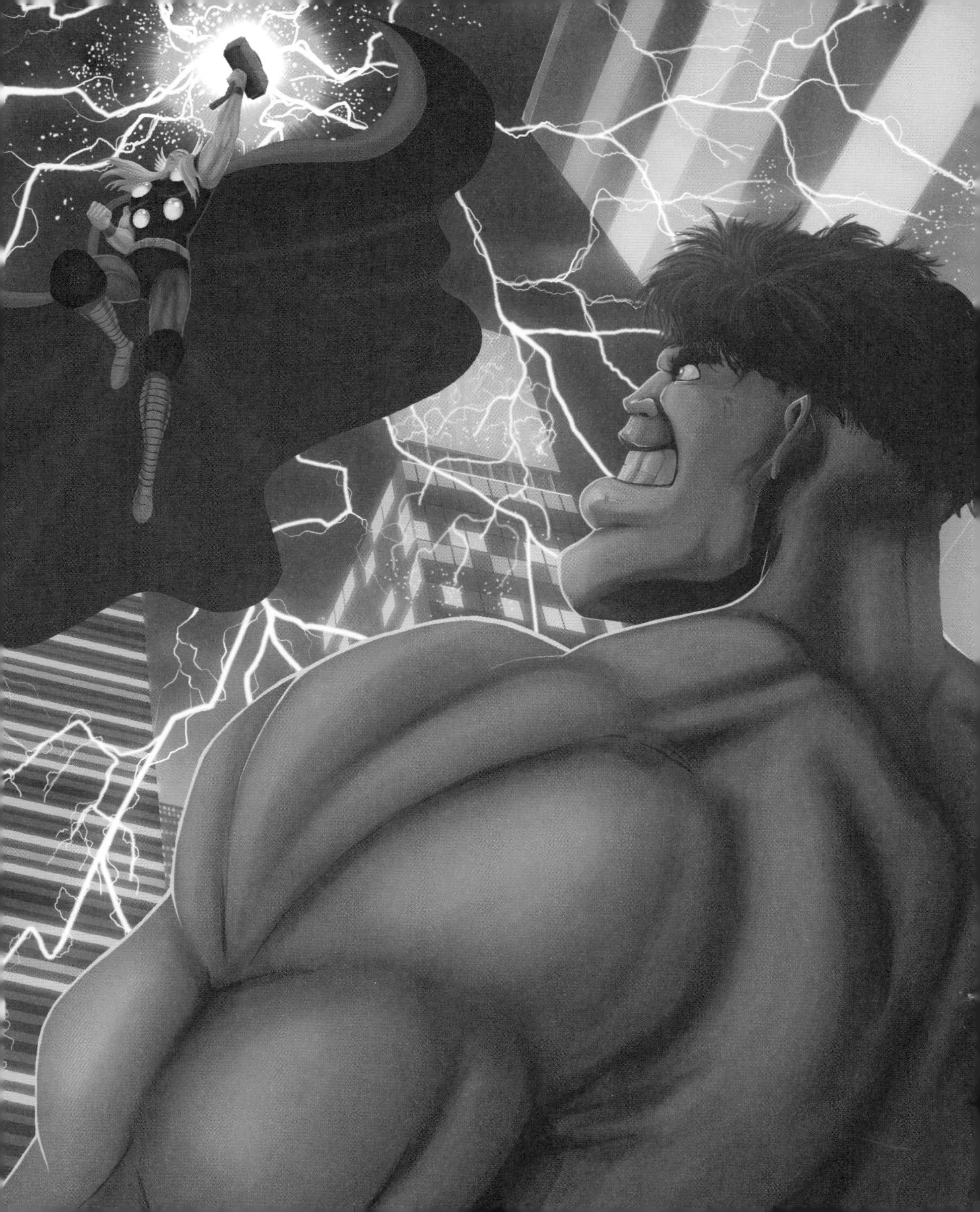

"The lights are on again in the city that never sleeps," said Captain America.

"Hulk like sleep," the green giant rumbled.

"Not now, Hulk. We've got a power plant to rebuild," Iron Man said. "Come on, Avengers."

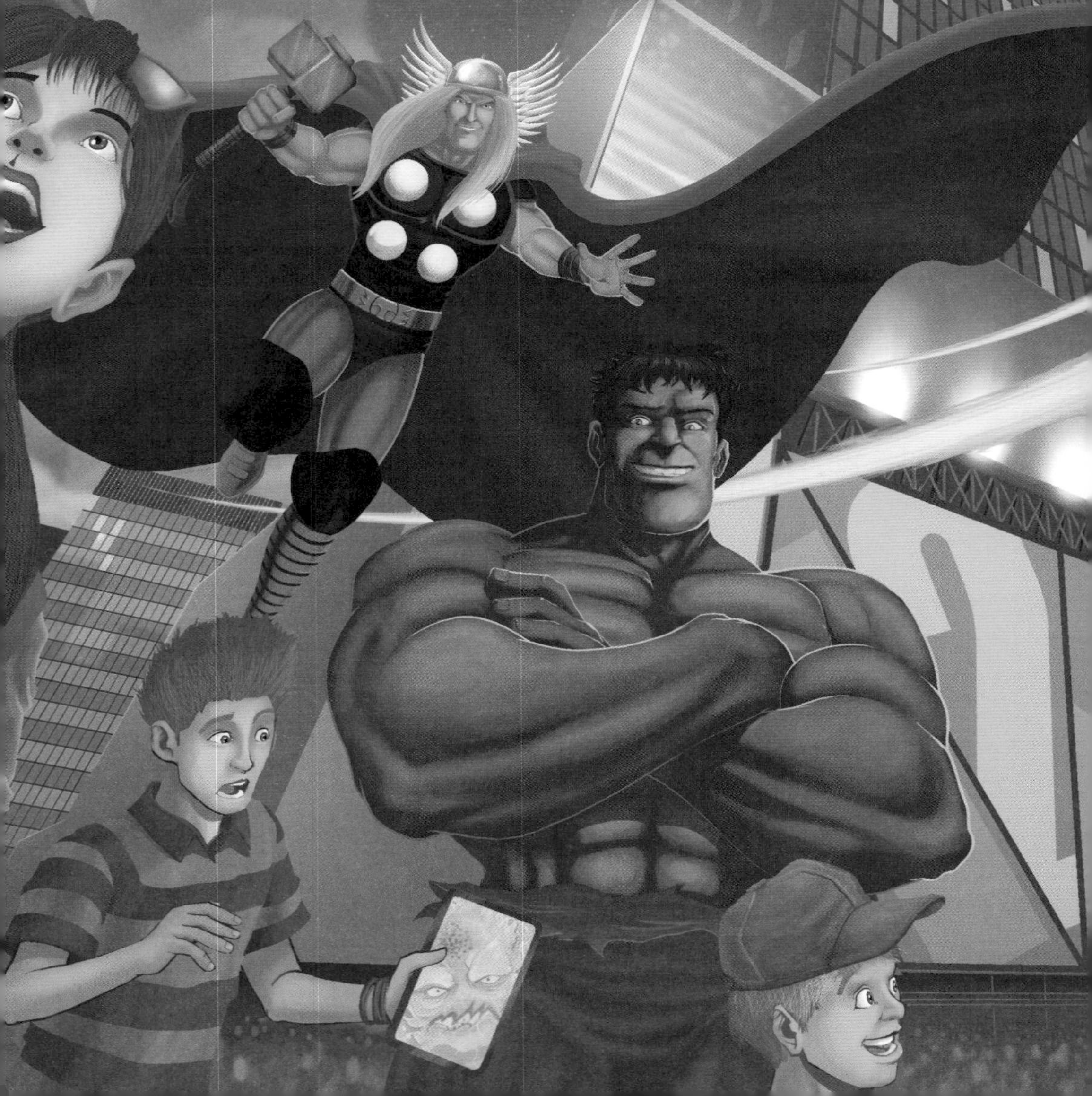

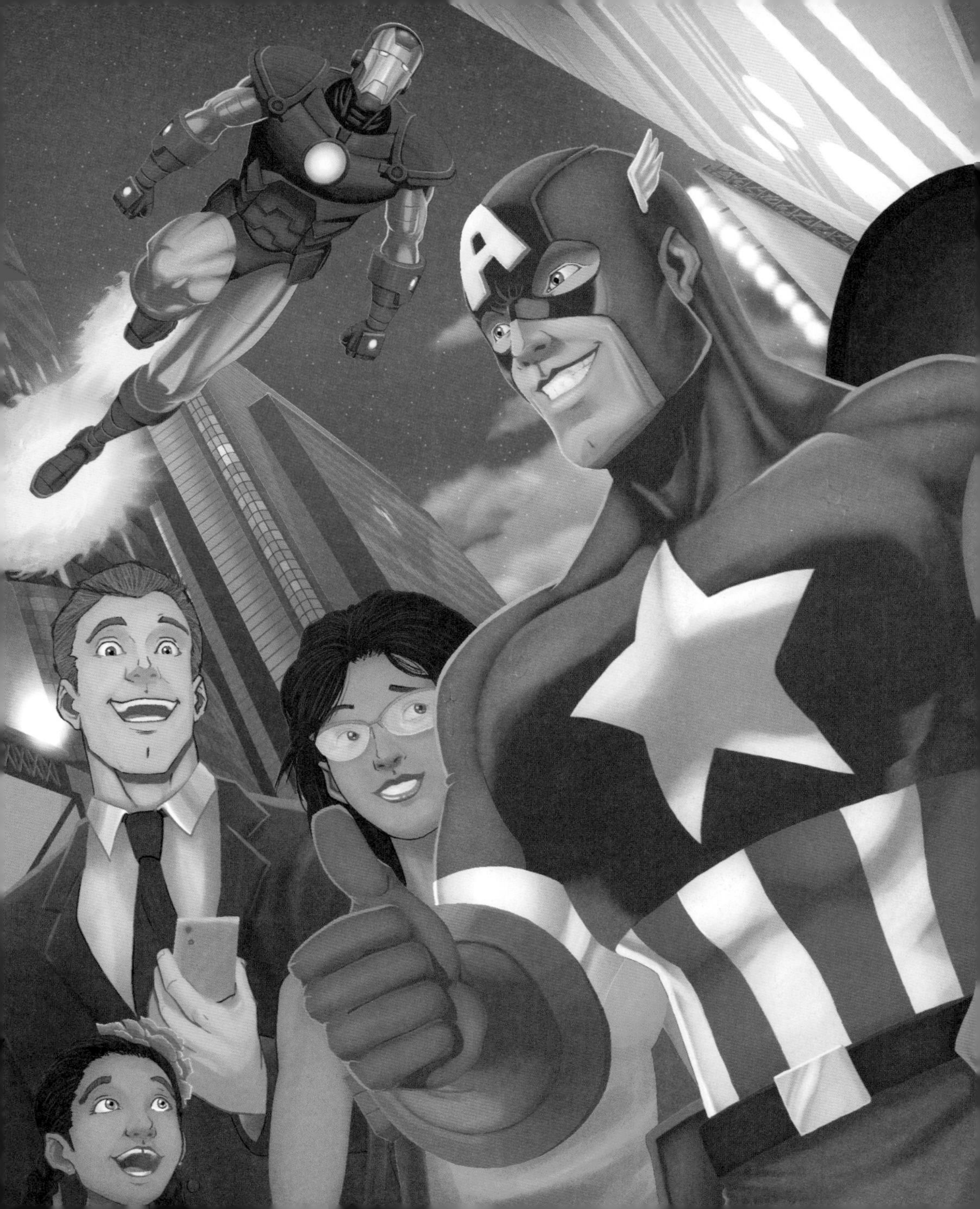

AVENGERS ASSEMBLE!

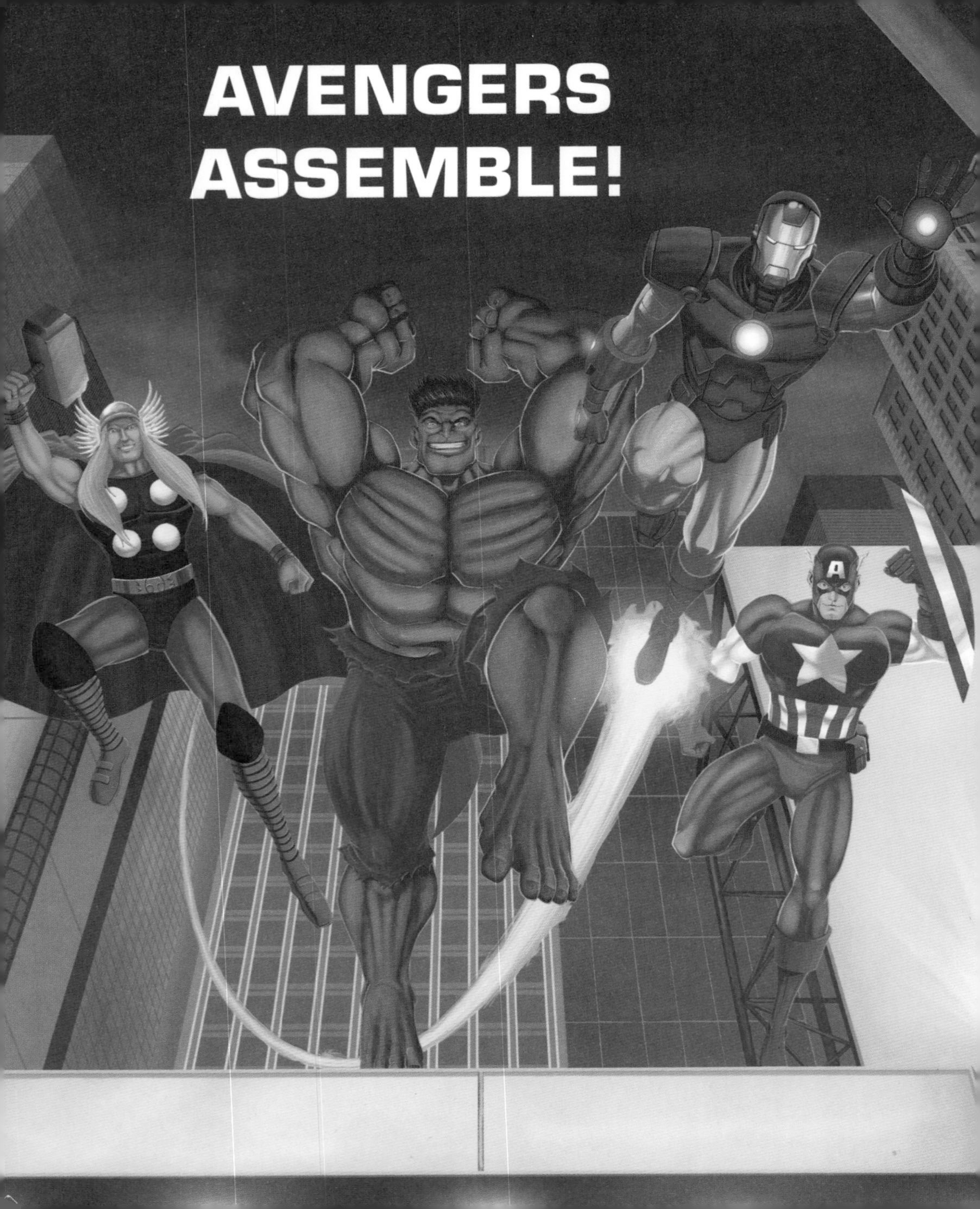

MARVEL AVENGERS

THUNDER STRIKE!

By John Sazaklis
Illustrated by Patrick Spaziante

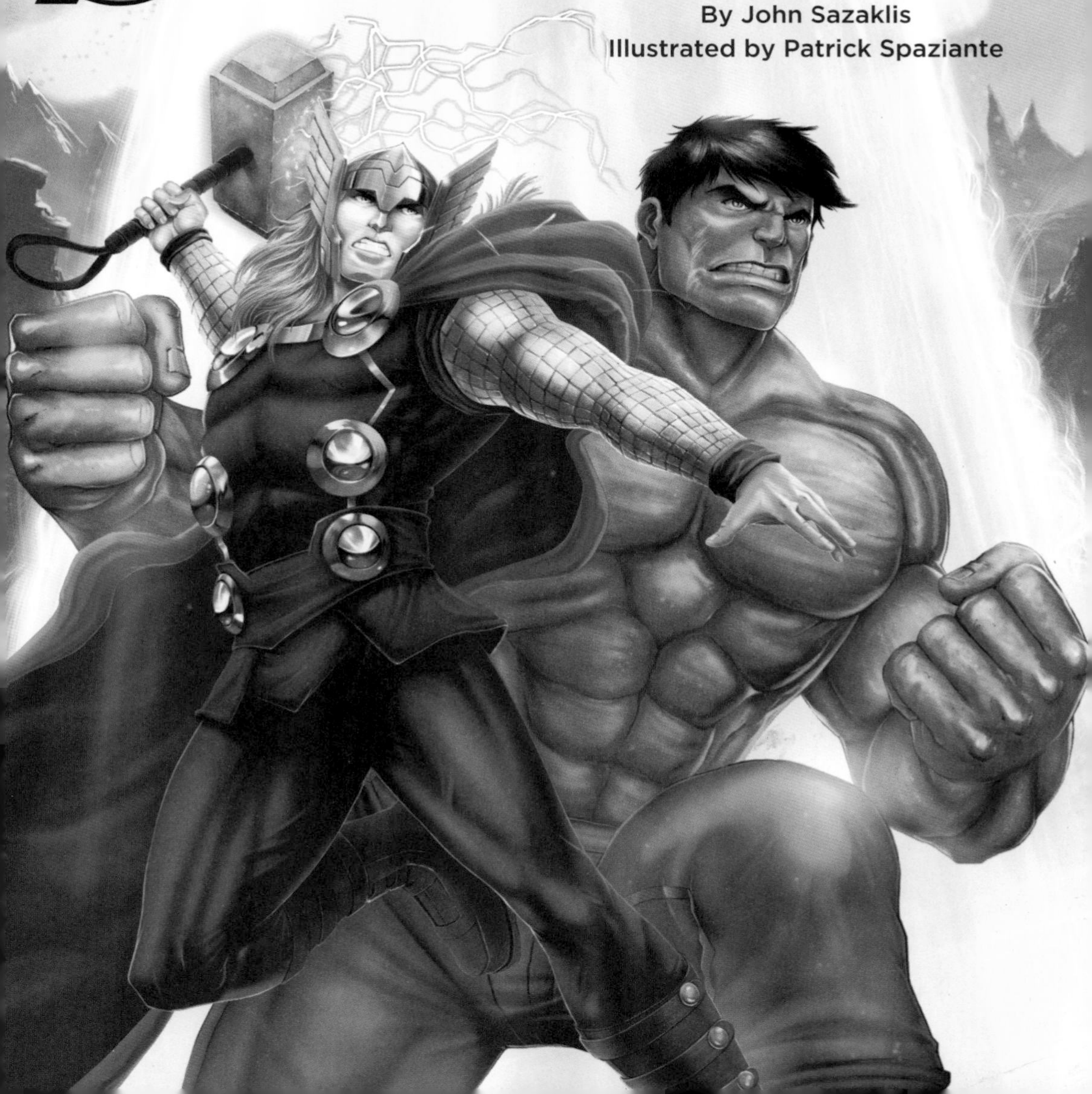

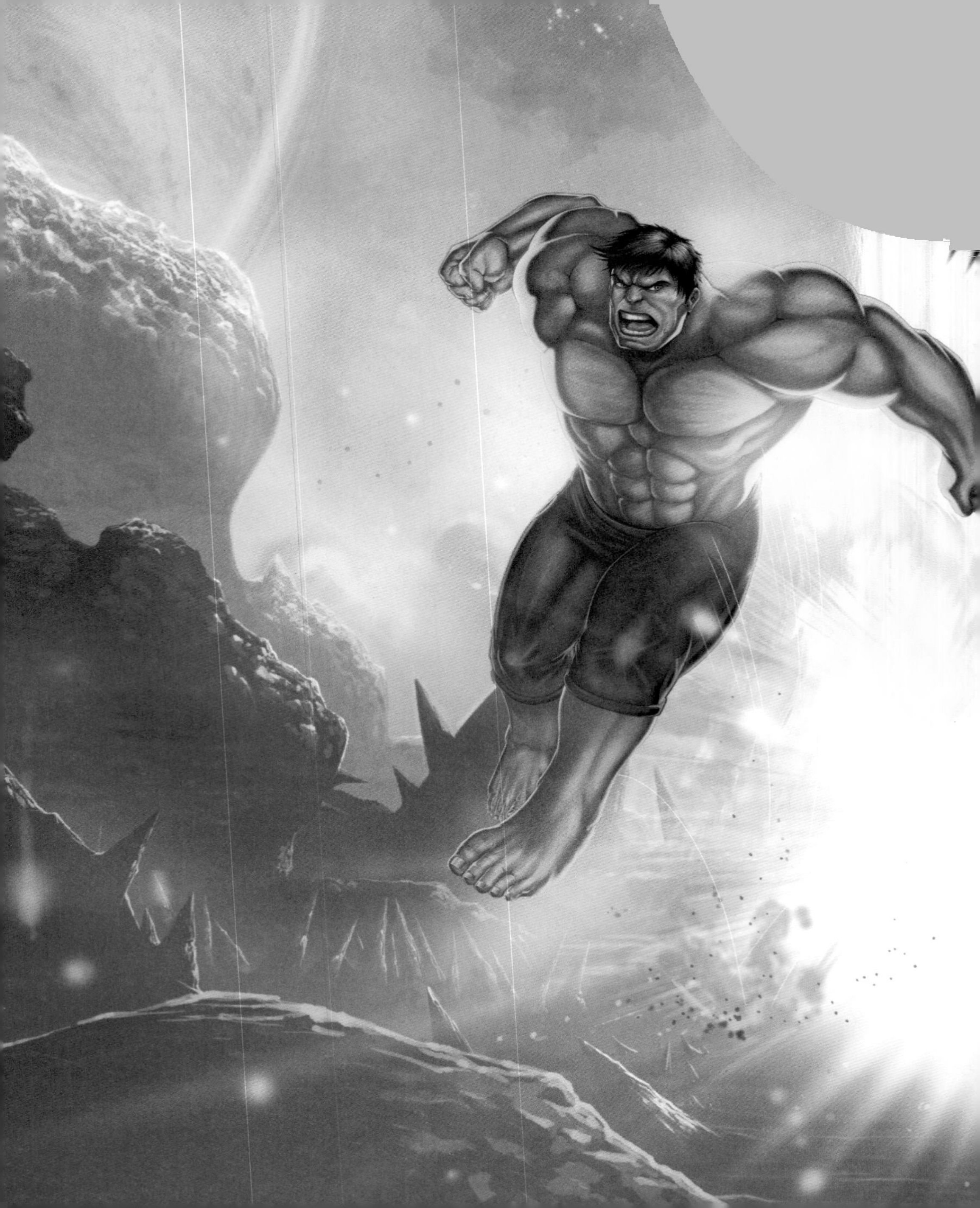

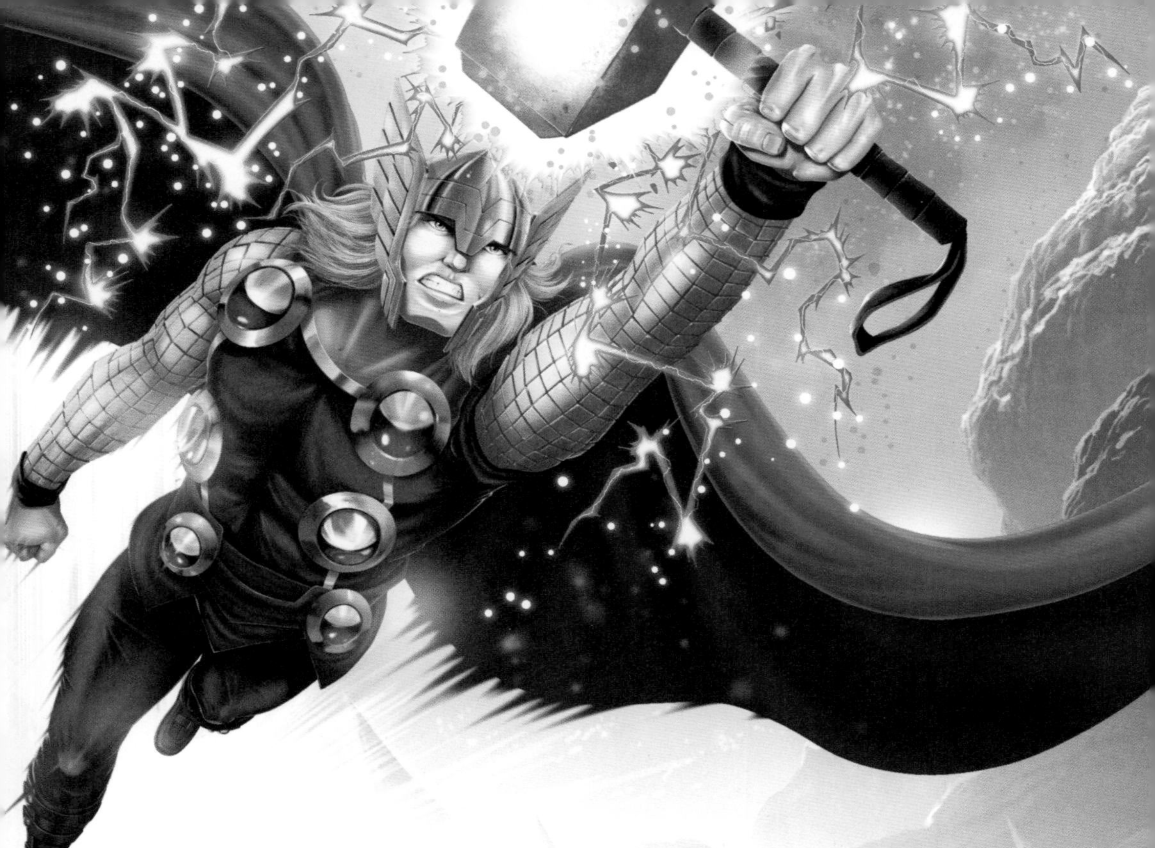

On a planet far from Earth, the hammer-wielding hero known as the **MIGHTY THOR** was searching for a stolen gem called the Moon Stone. Giant rock warriors known as the Kronans had taken it.

"Onward!" Thor shouted to his fellow Avenger the **INCREDIBLE HULK**.

The Moon Stone was guarded by a group of Kronans and surrounded by a super-charged force field.

"HULK SMASH!" the Hulk roared.

"Wait!" Thor cried, but it was too late.

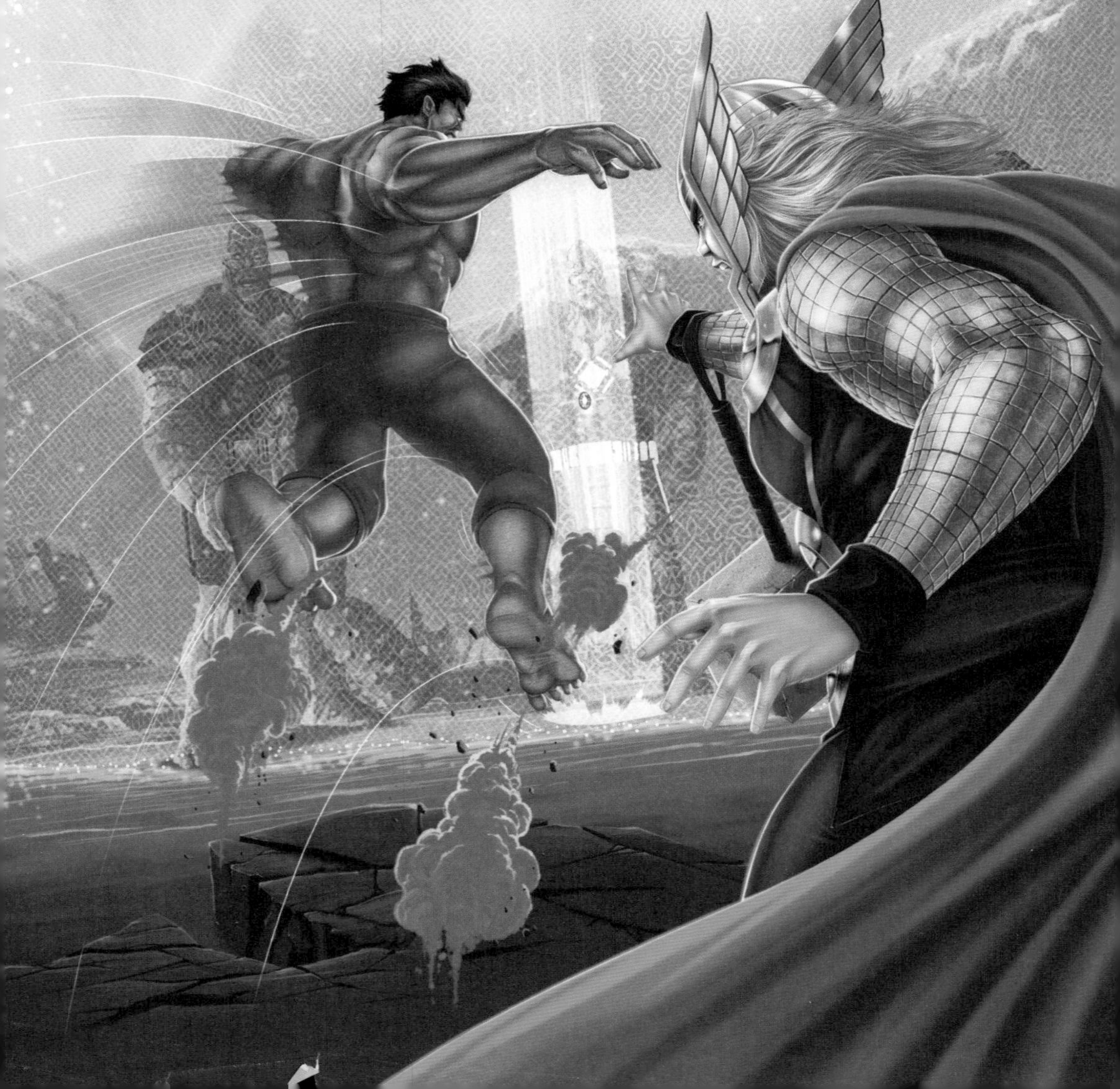

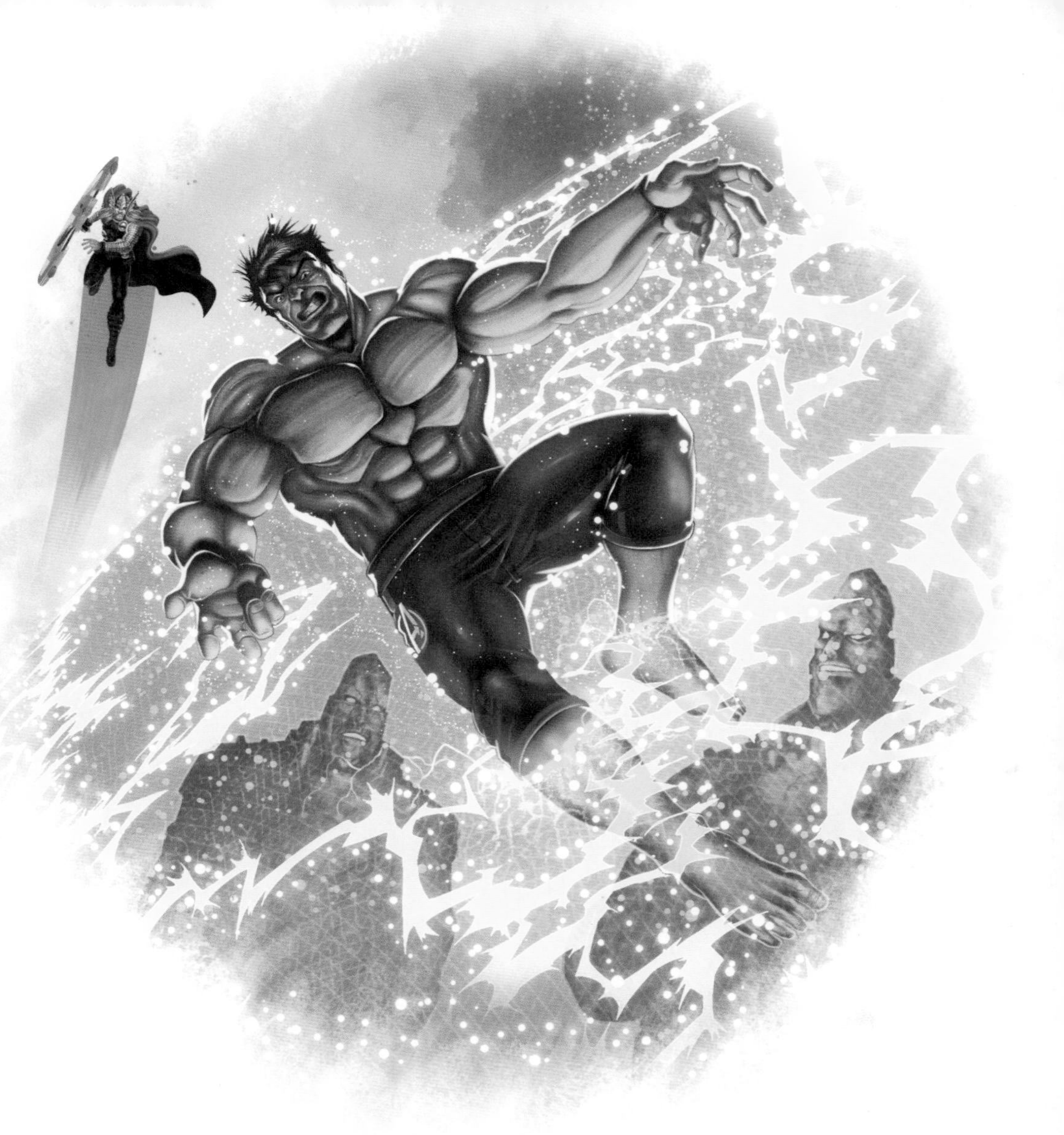

Hulk punched the force field and got a shocking surprise!

ZZZZARK!

"'Twas a noble effort, friend," said Thor. "But nothing can withstand my mighty hammer!"

Thor launched himself through the force field and barreled into the Kronans.

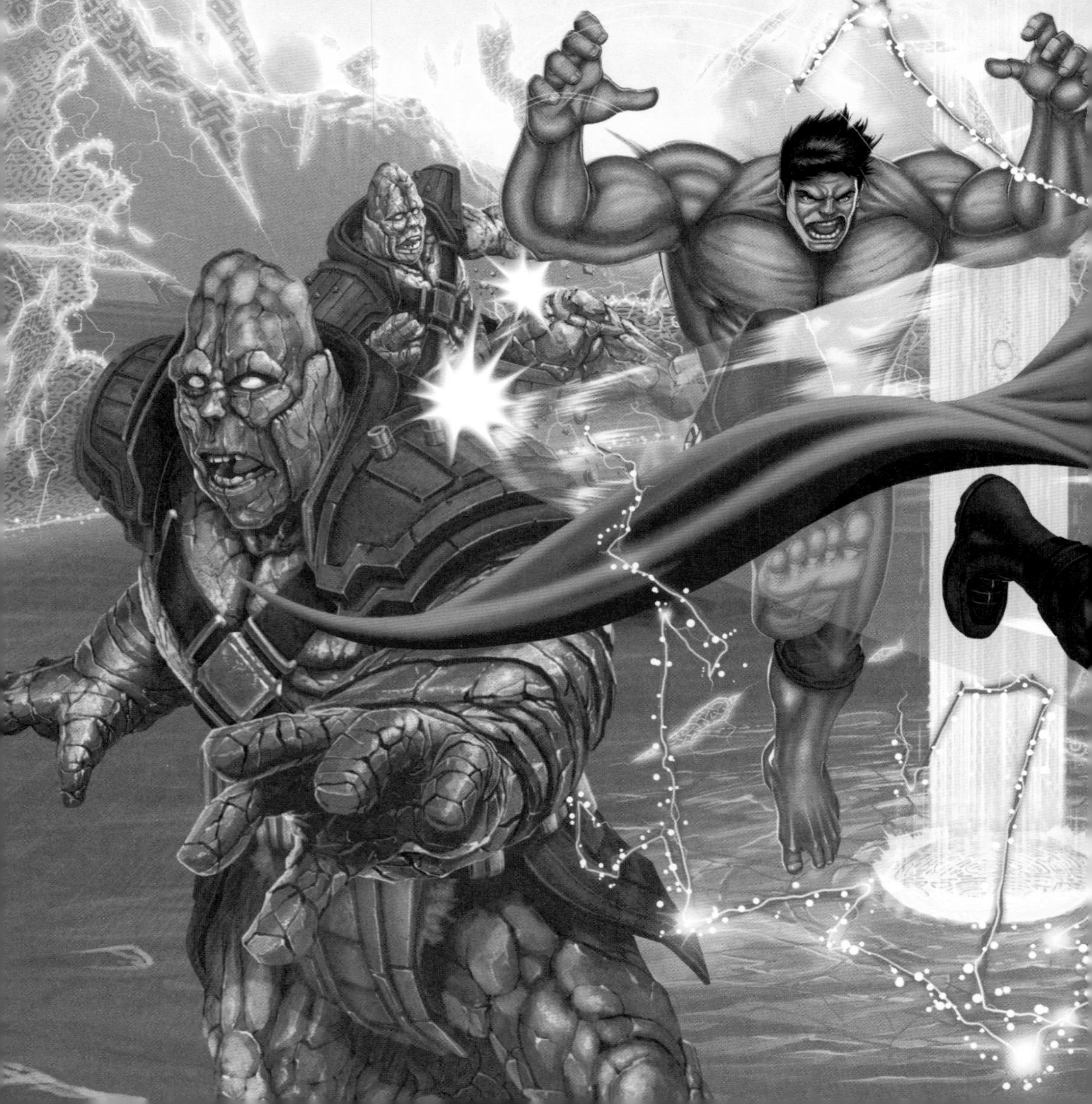

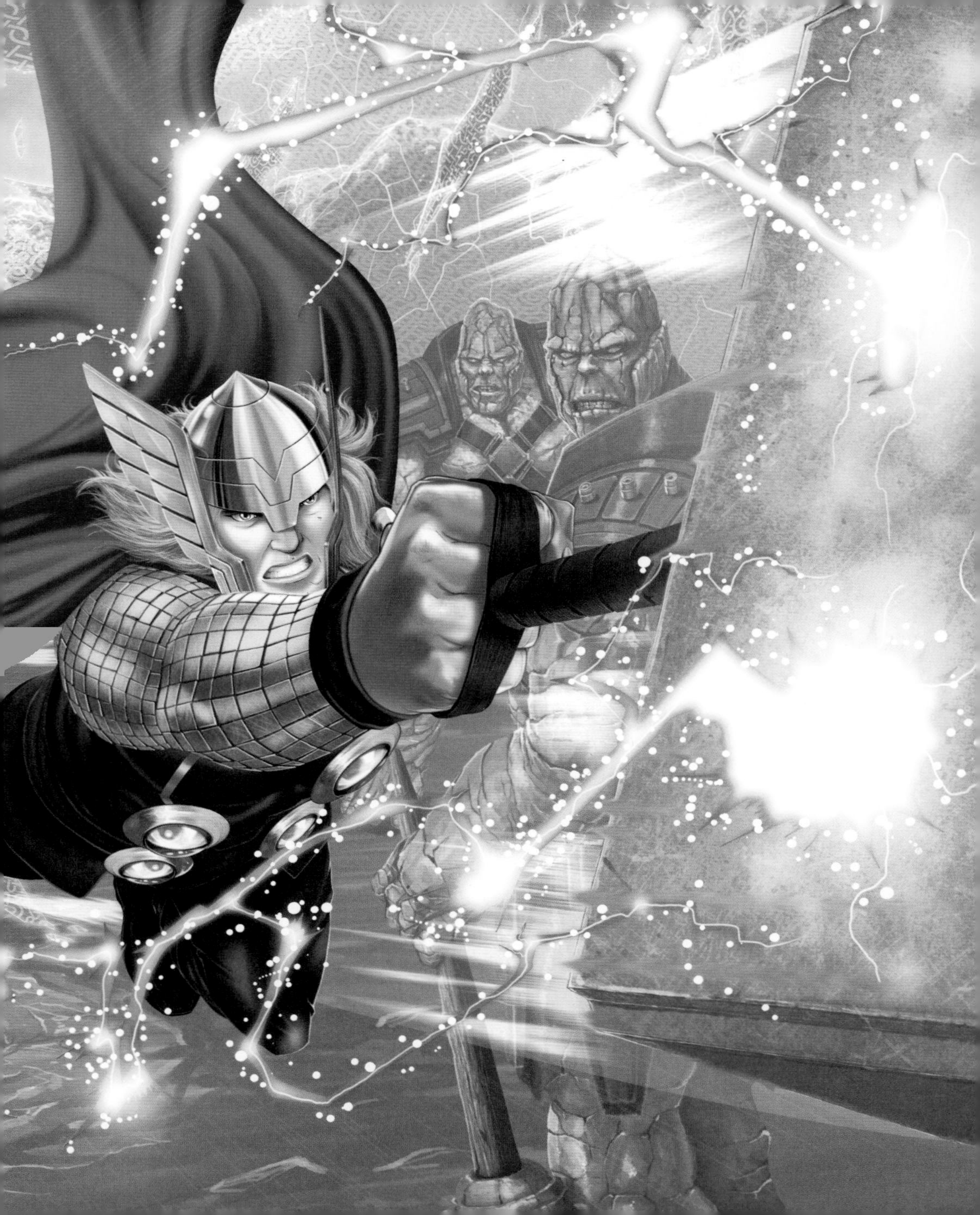

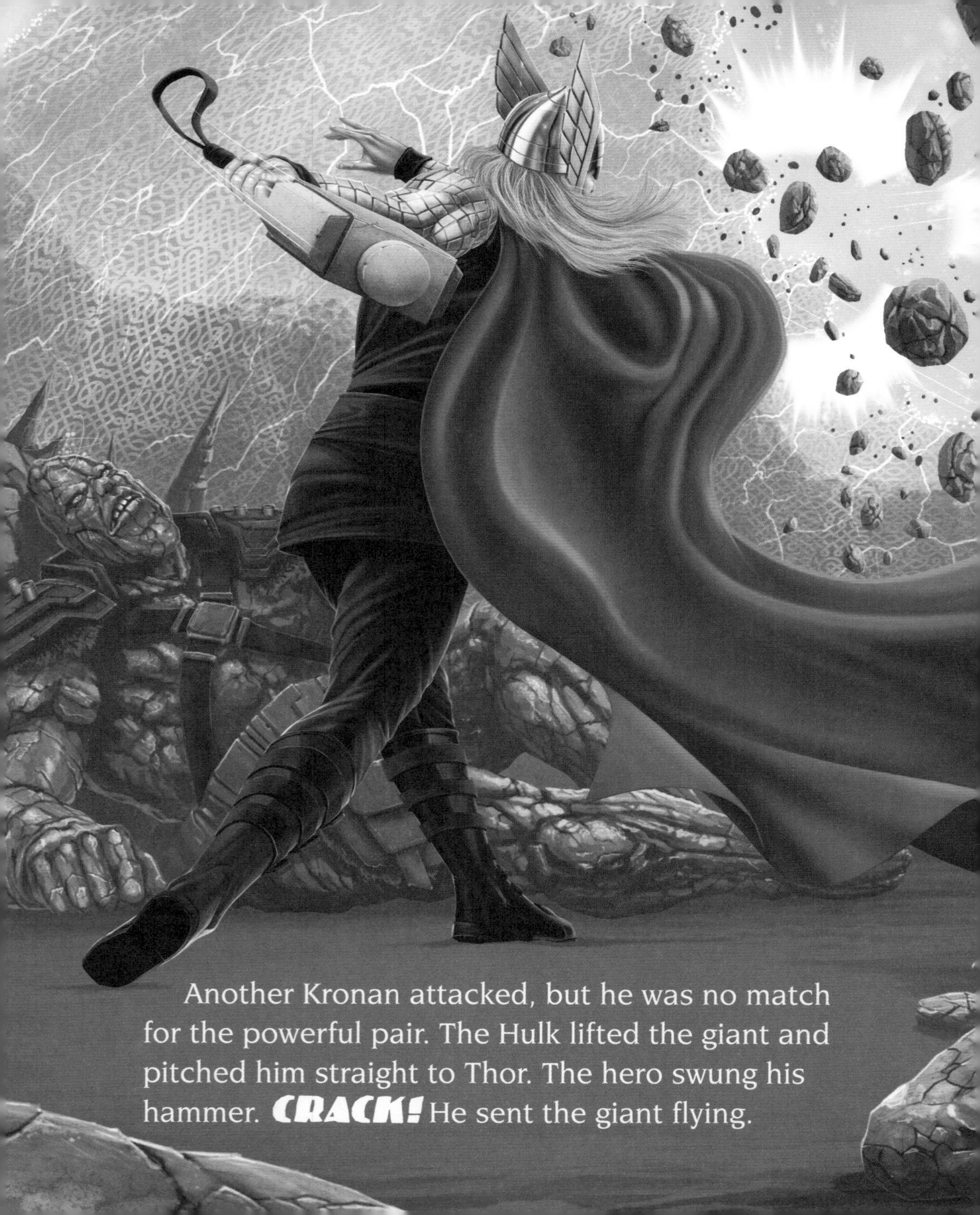

Another Kronan attacked, but he was no match for the powerful pair. The Hulk lifted the giant and pitched him straight to Thor. The hero swung his hammer. **CRACK!** He sent the giant flying.

Thor and Hulk quickly turned the rest of the rock monsters to piles of rubble.

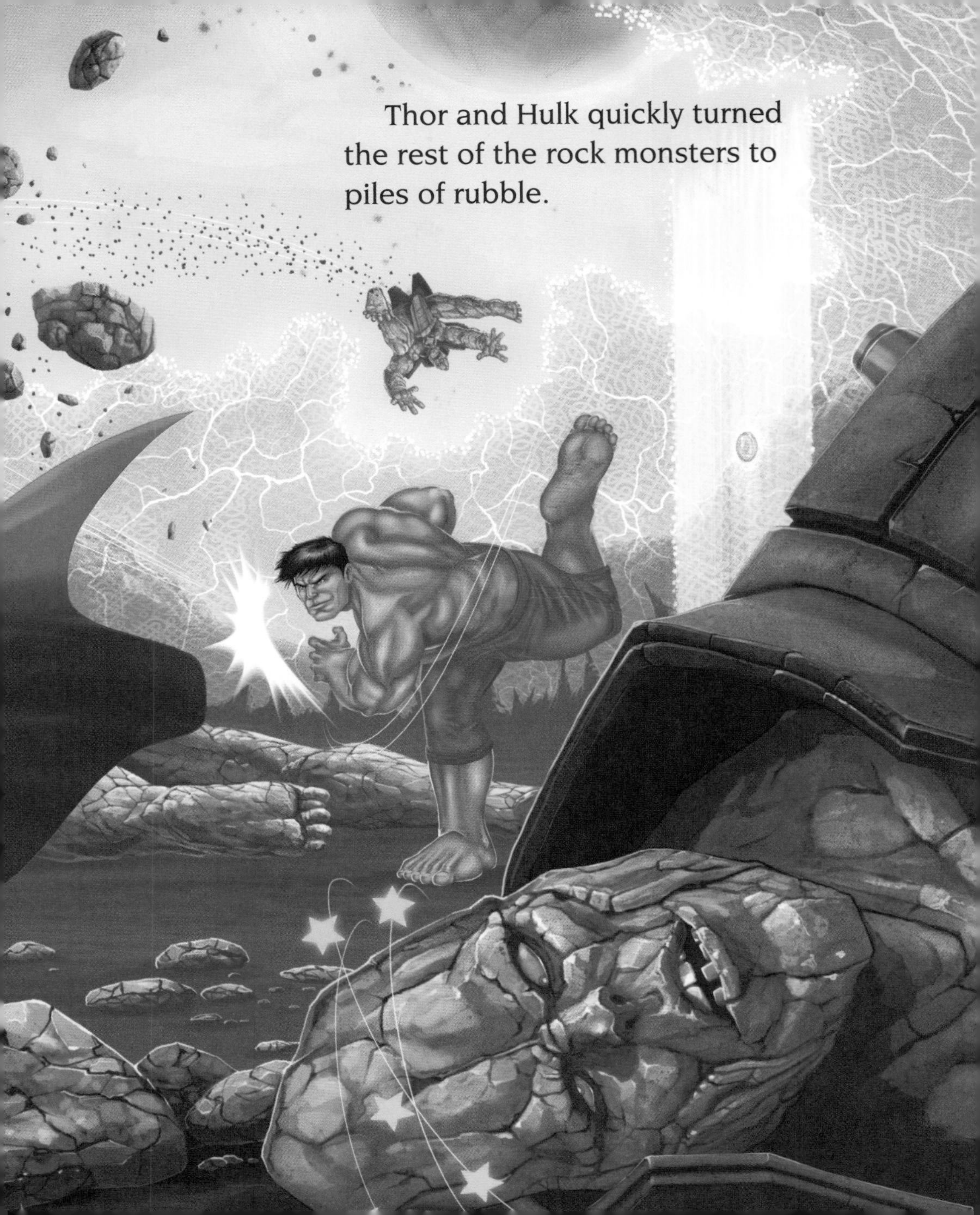

Little did the heroes know, the cosmic villain ***GRANDMASTER*** was watching.

"Those muscle-bound buffoons have beaten me to the Moon Stone," Grandmaster grumbled. "But I'll beat them to the punch!"

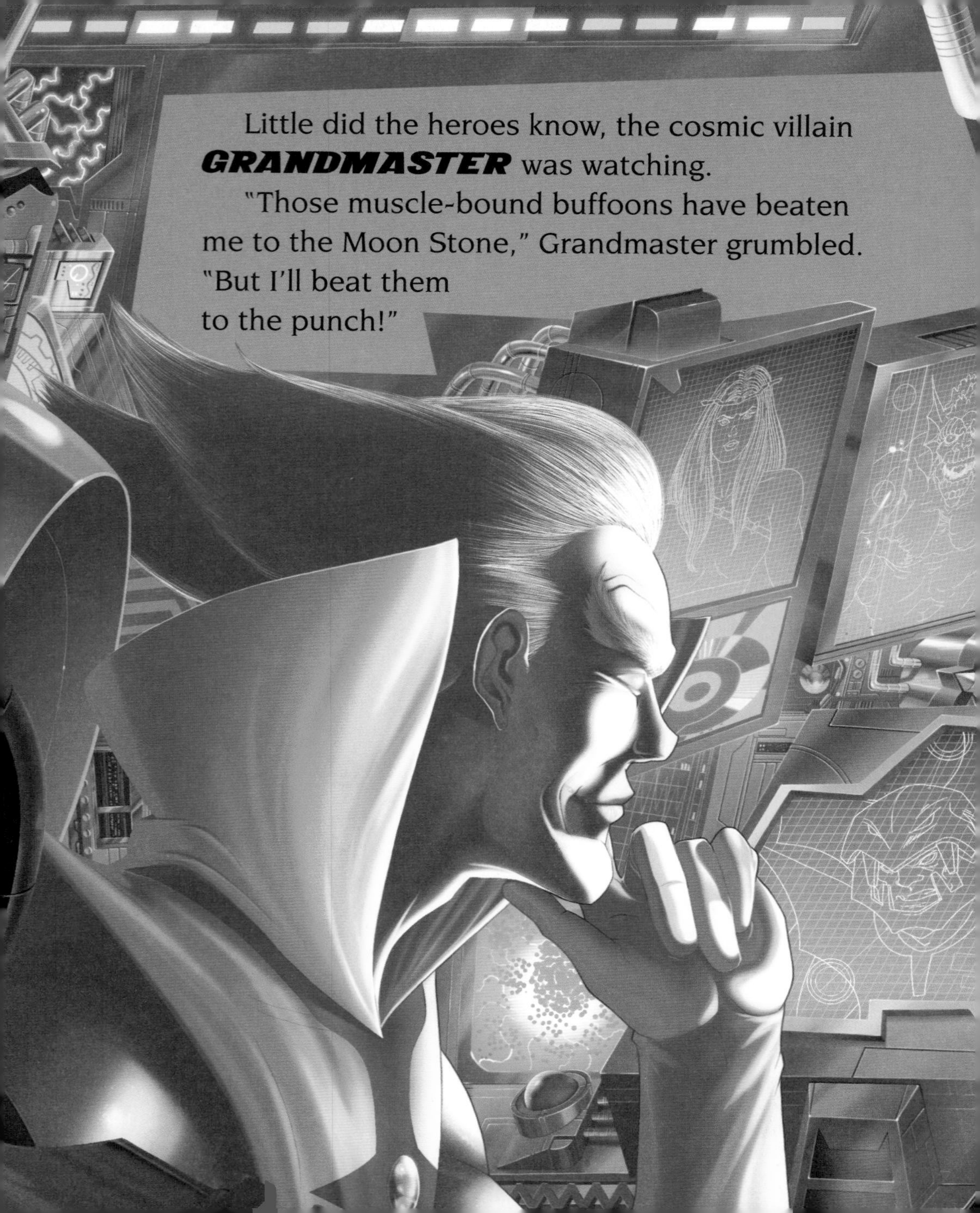

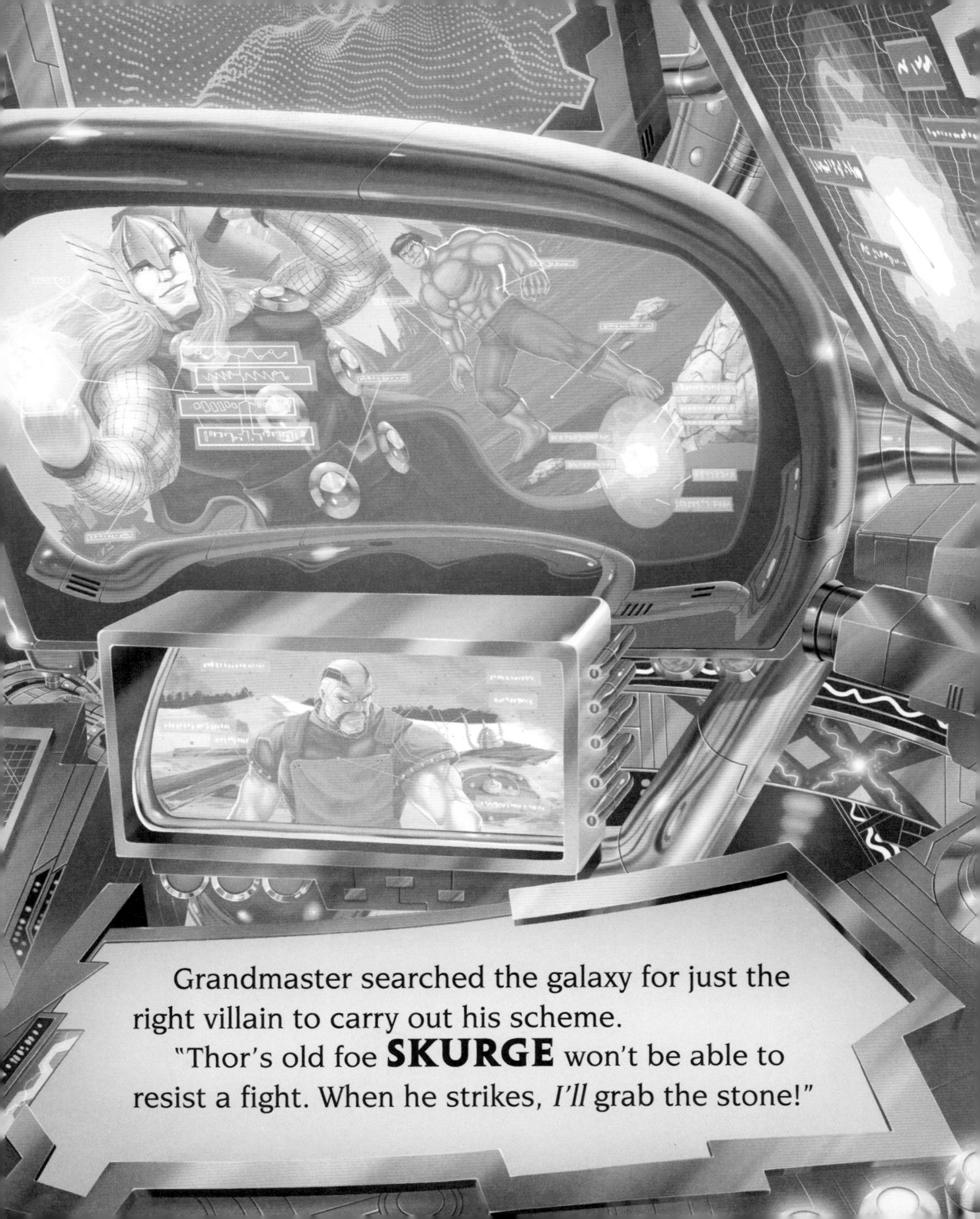

Grandmaster searched the galaxy for just the right villain to carry out his scheme.

"Thor's old foe **SKURGE** won't be able to resist a fight. When he strikes, *I'll* grab the stone!"

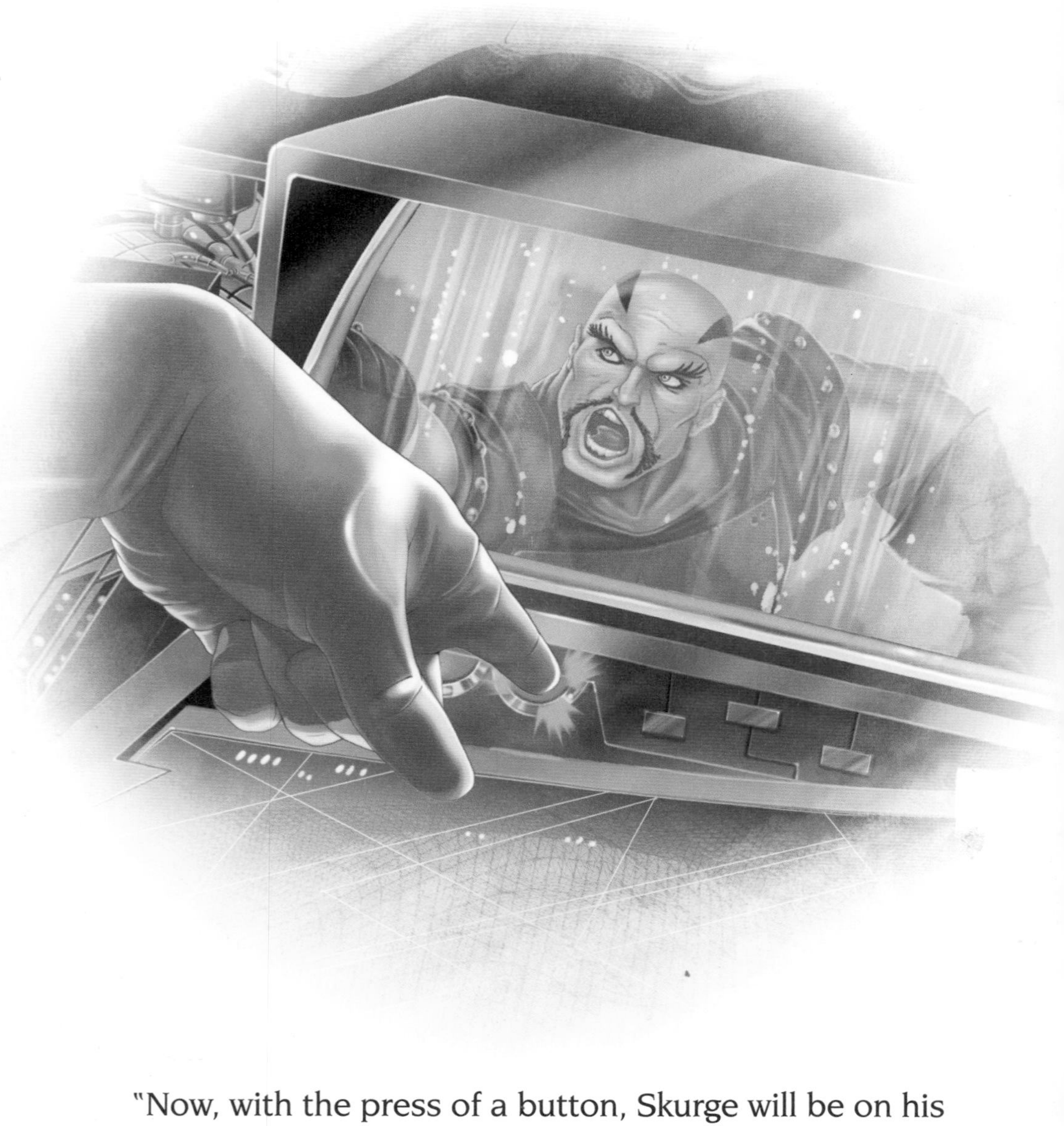

"Now, with the press of a button, Skurge will be on his way!" Grandmaster said. He opened a portal, transporting the ax-wielding villain across the cosmos . . .

. . . to confront the heroes.

"Thor! This must be my lucky day," Skurge growled, ready to fight. "I've got an ax to grind with you."

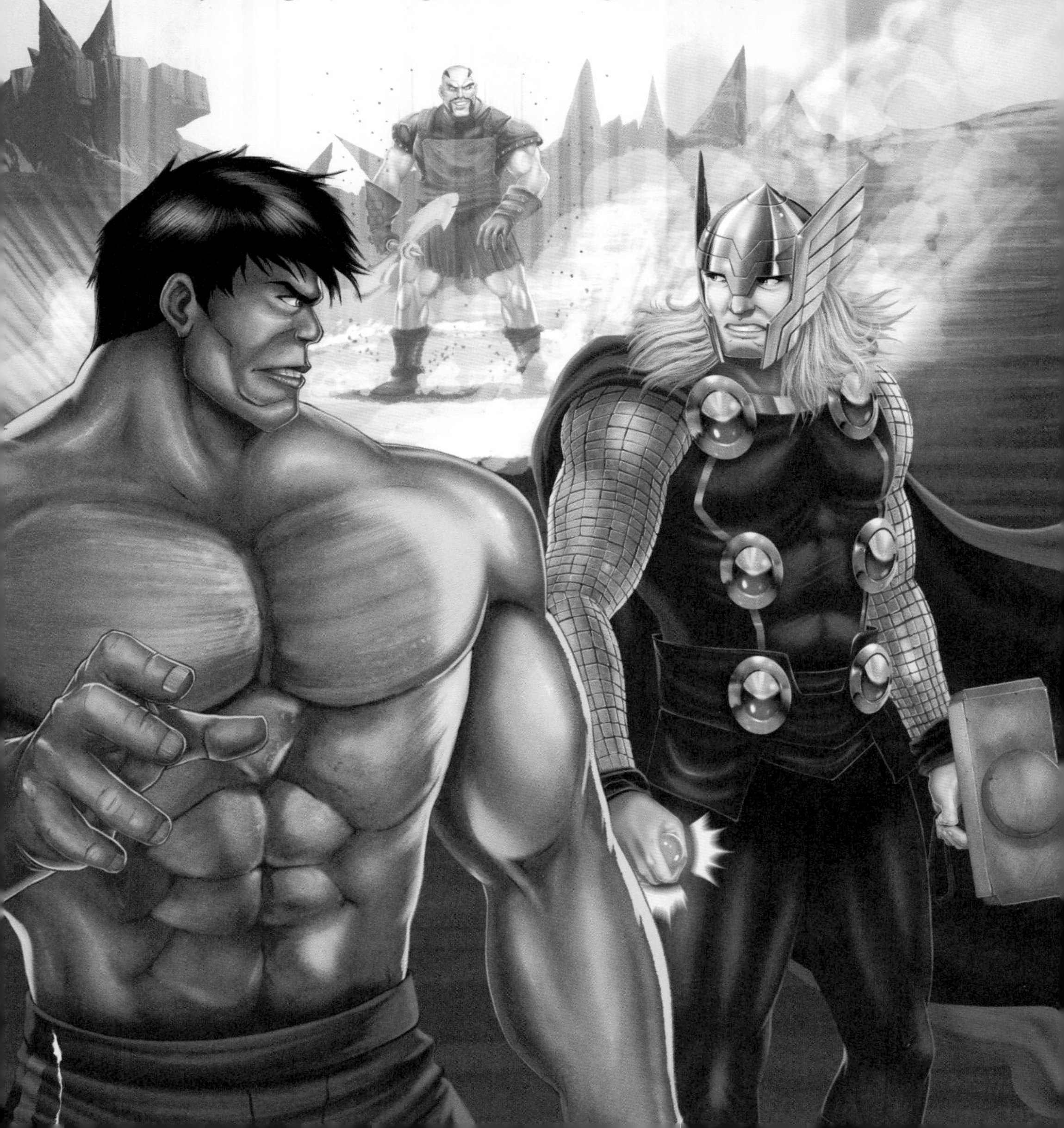

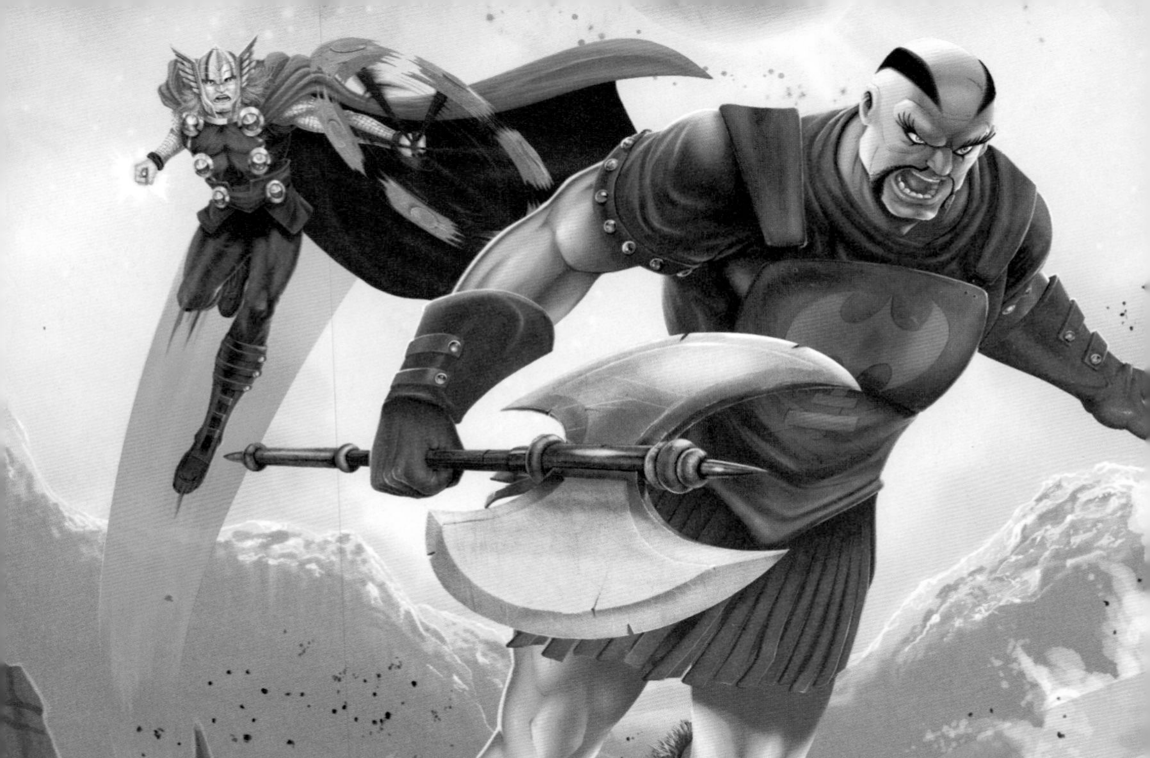

"Skurge!" Thor exclaimed. "Thy presence is most unwelcome!"

"I don't know who sent me here," Skurge snarled. "But I'll deal with *them* as soon as I'm done with *you*."

"Hulk smash big man with puny ax!" Hulk roared.

"Careful, Hulk," Thor cautioned. "Skurge is as strong as he is treacherous. He is mine to face."

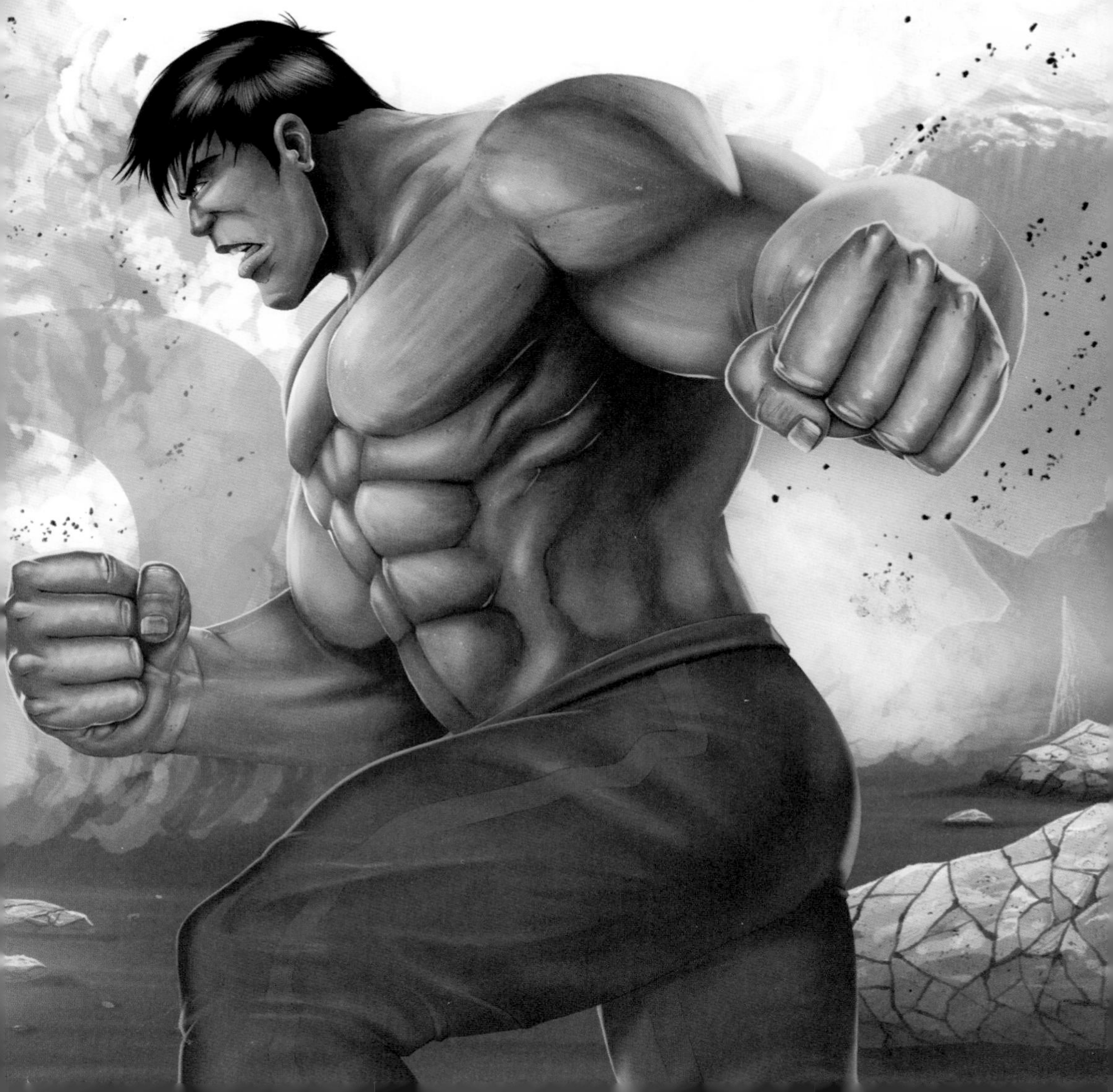

The air crackled with electricity—***ZZZZ!***—as Thor and Skurge clashed, hammer against ax! The power they unleashed held even the massive Hulk back.

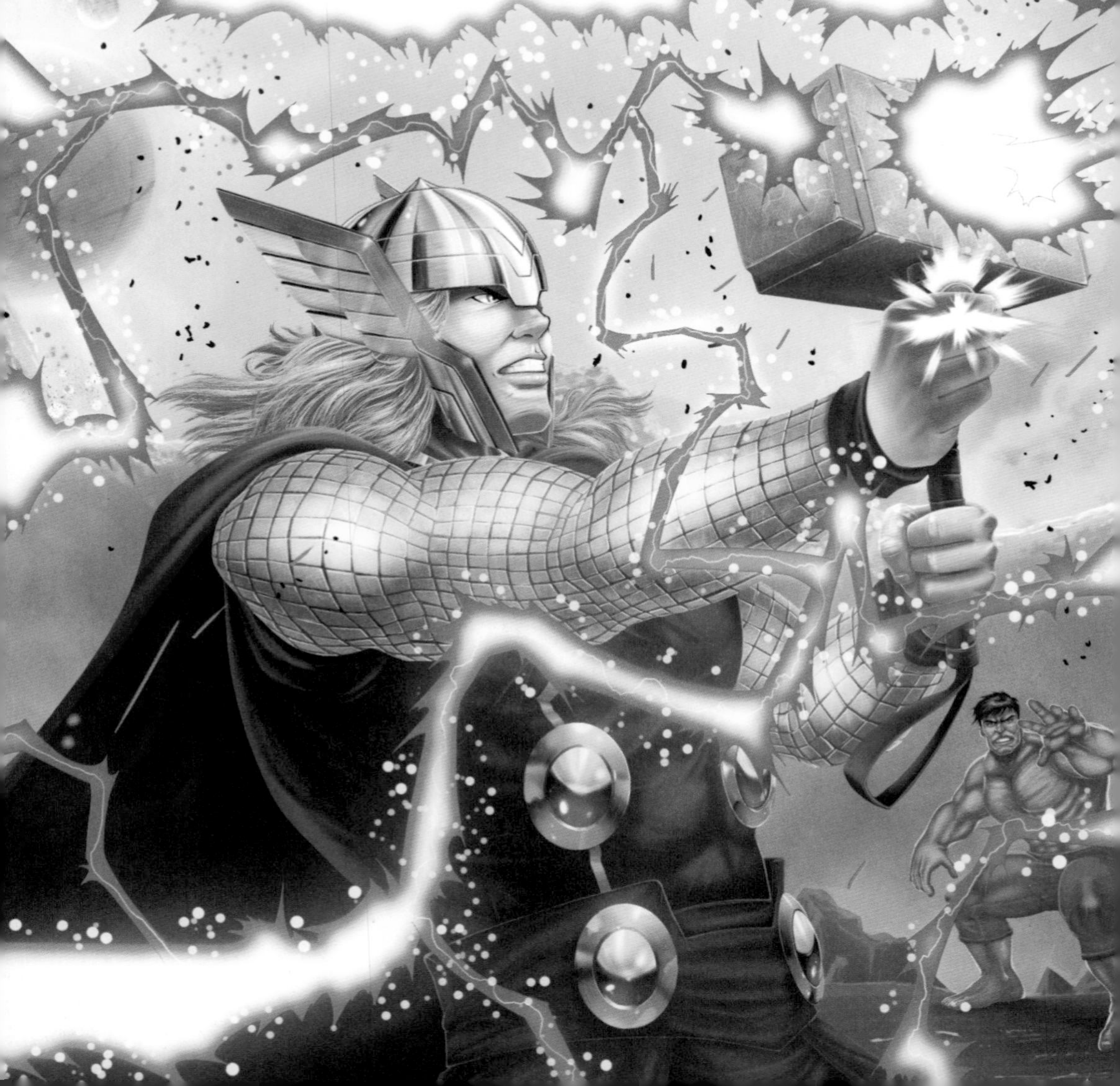

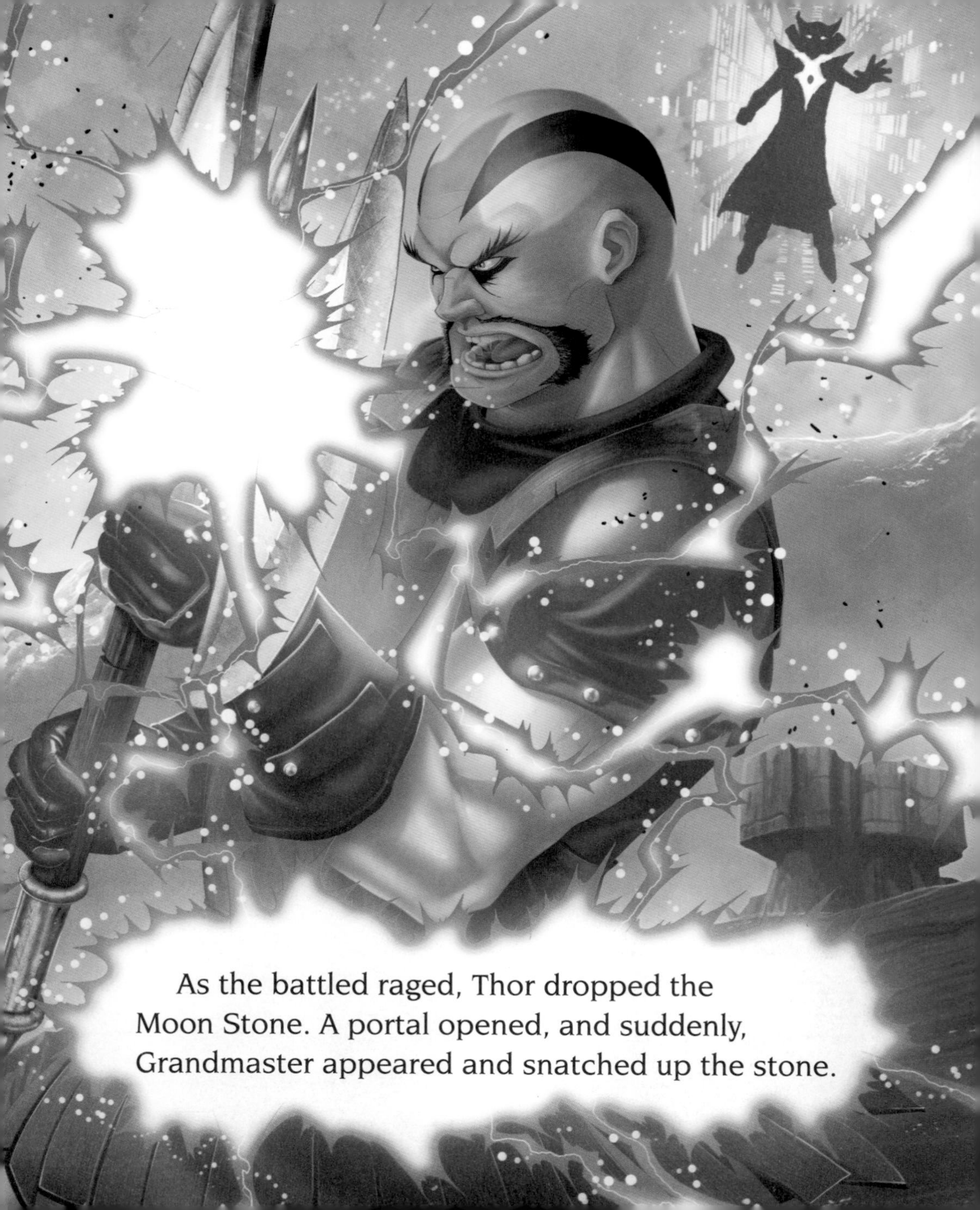

As the battled raged, Thor dropped the Moon Stone. A portal opened, and suddenly, Grandmaster appeared and snatched up the stone.

"It is all mine!" Grandmaster boasted as he blasted Thor in the back with a beam of energy.

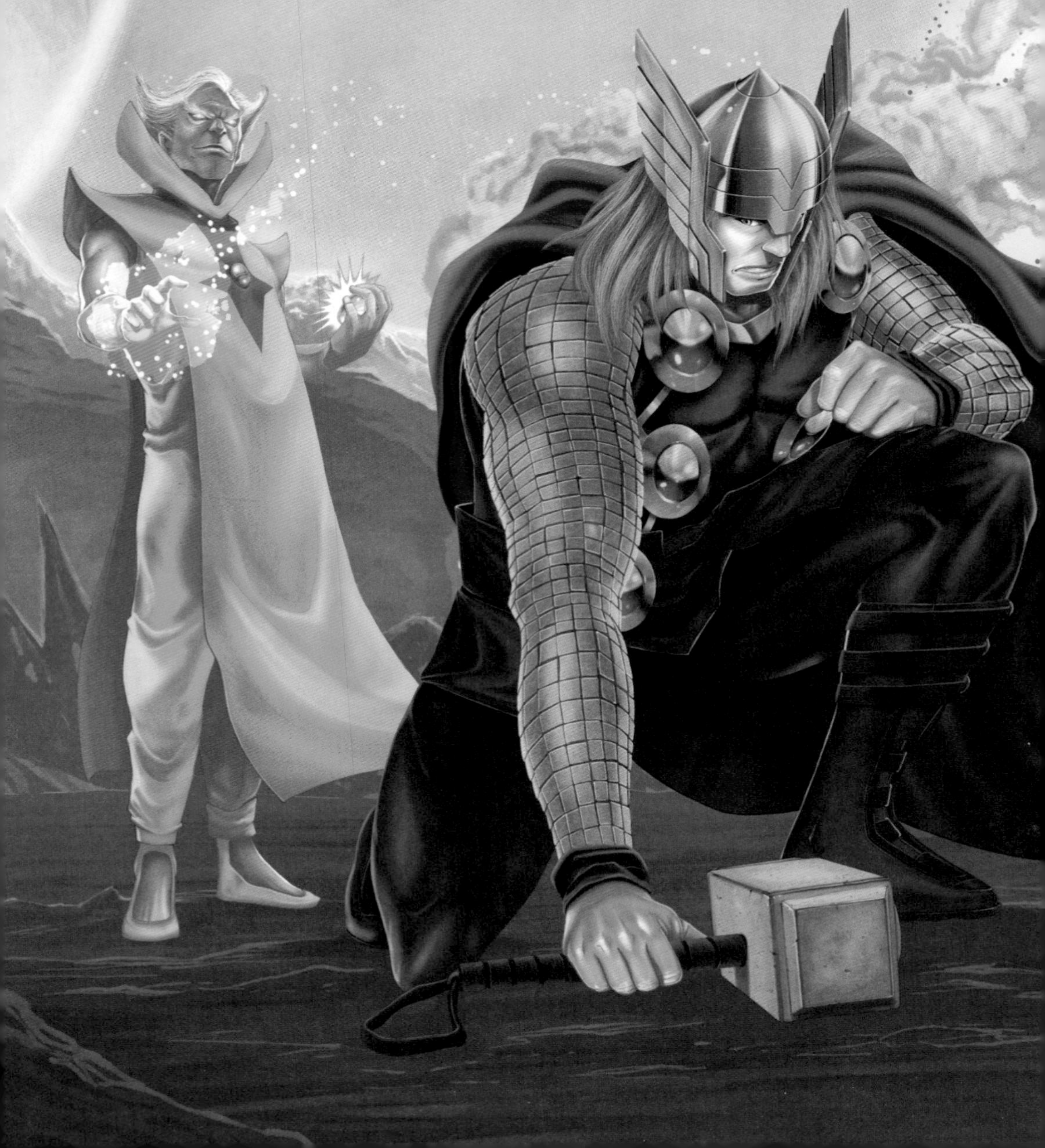

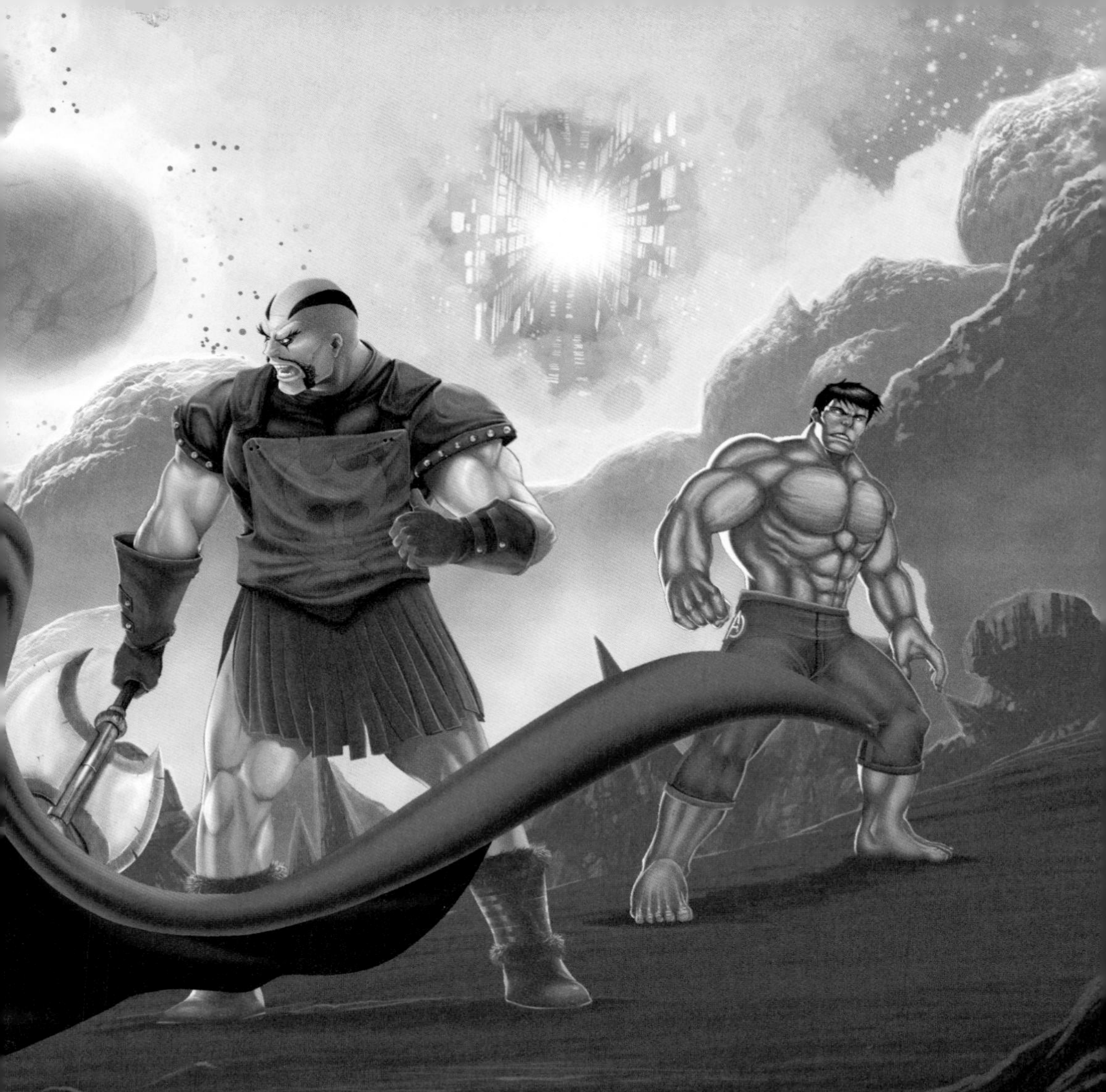

"I think someone has played you for a fool," Thor told Skurge.

"If that shiny rock belongs to anyone, old man, it's *me*!" Skurge growled as he turned to Grandmaster. "I did all the fighting."

"Stay back!" Grandmaster cried, and he turned to run to the open portal. The Hulk slammed his massive foot on the ground. The earth quaked, and both villains were sent tumbling.

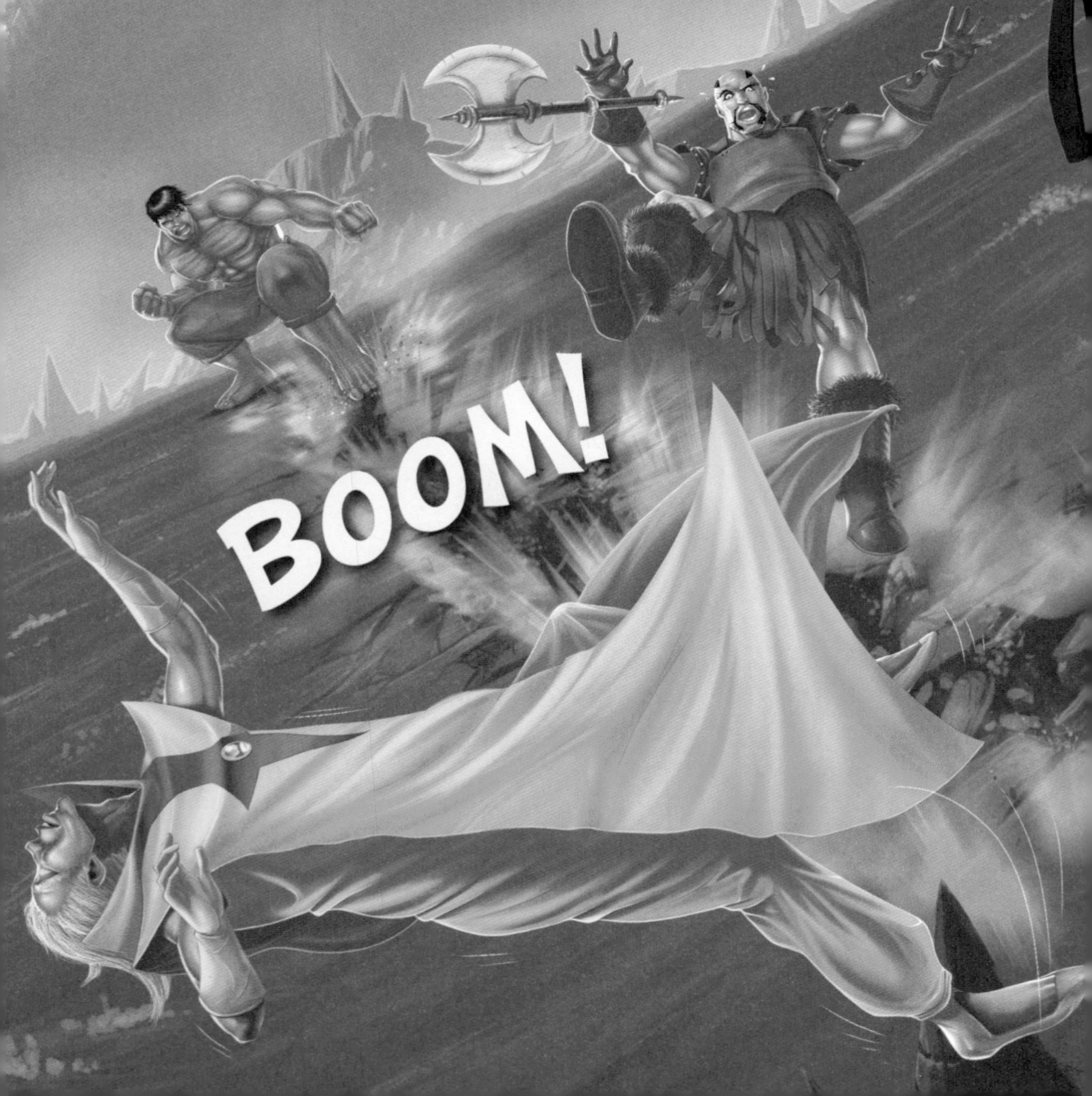
BOOM!

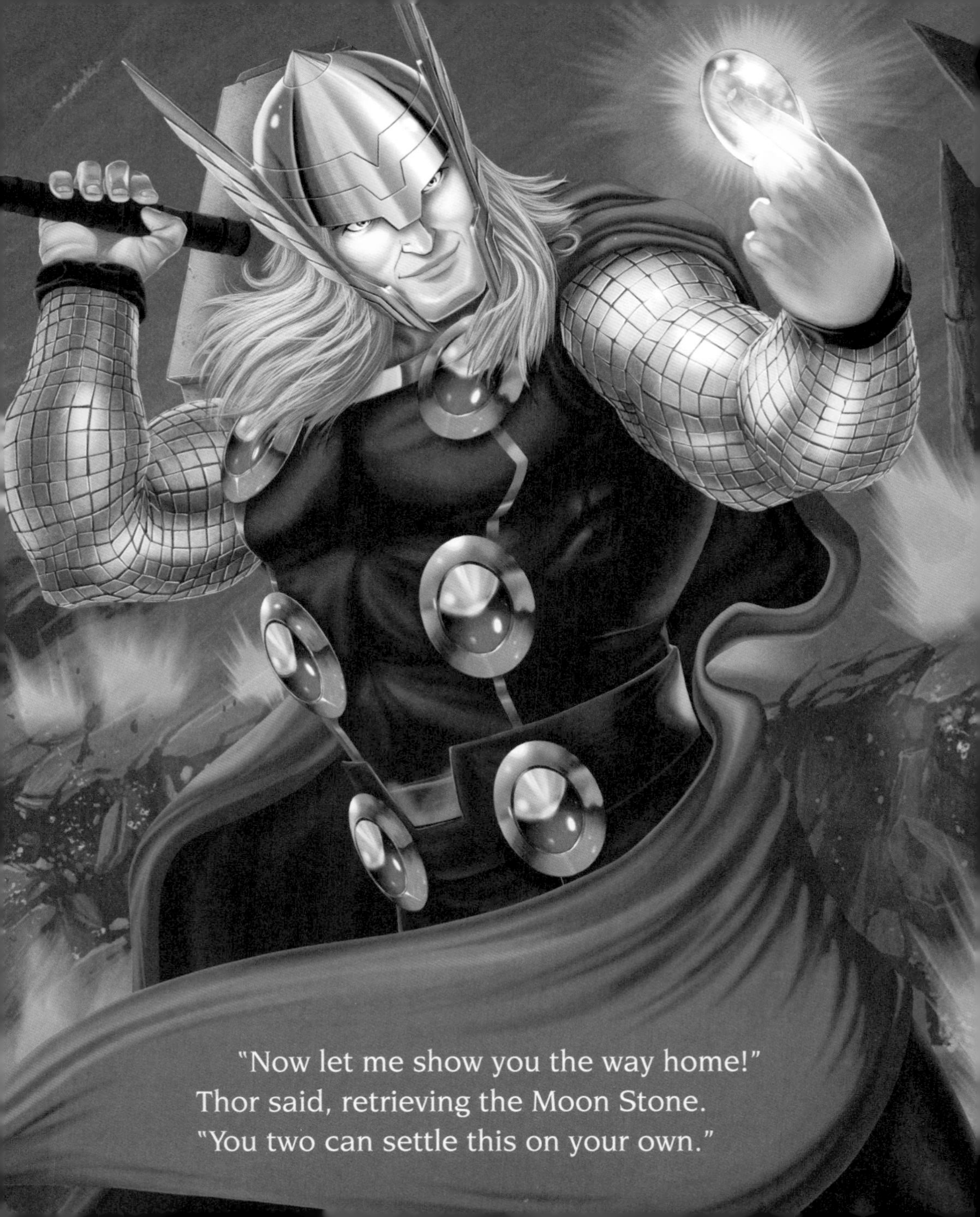

"Now let me show you the way home!" Thor said, retrieving the Moon Stone. "You two can settle this on your own."

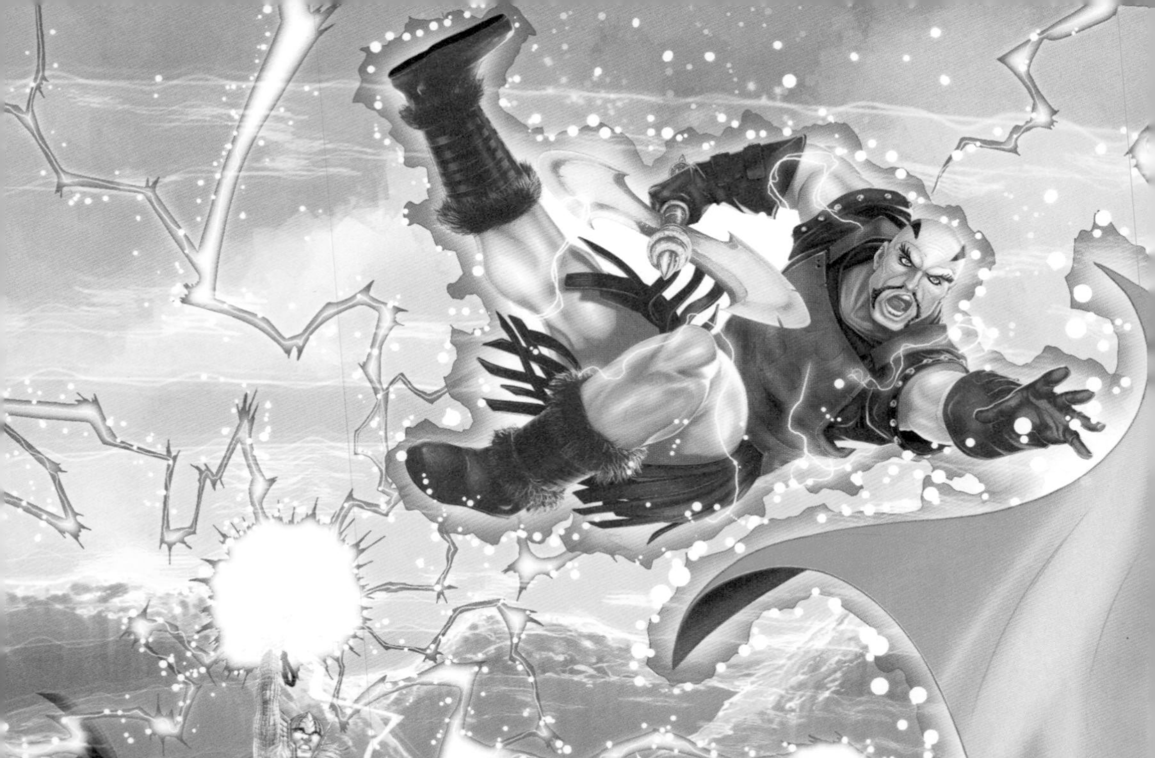

The blond warrior called forth a powerful bolt of lightning that blasted Grandmaster and Skurge toward an open portal. The villains tried to resist, but . . .

. . . the Hulk slapped his mighty hands together, creating a sonic boom that hurled them onward.

Then another bolt of lightning from Thor's hammer closed the portal for good!

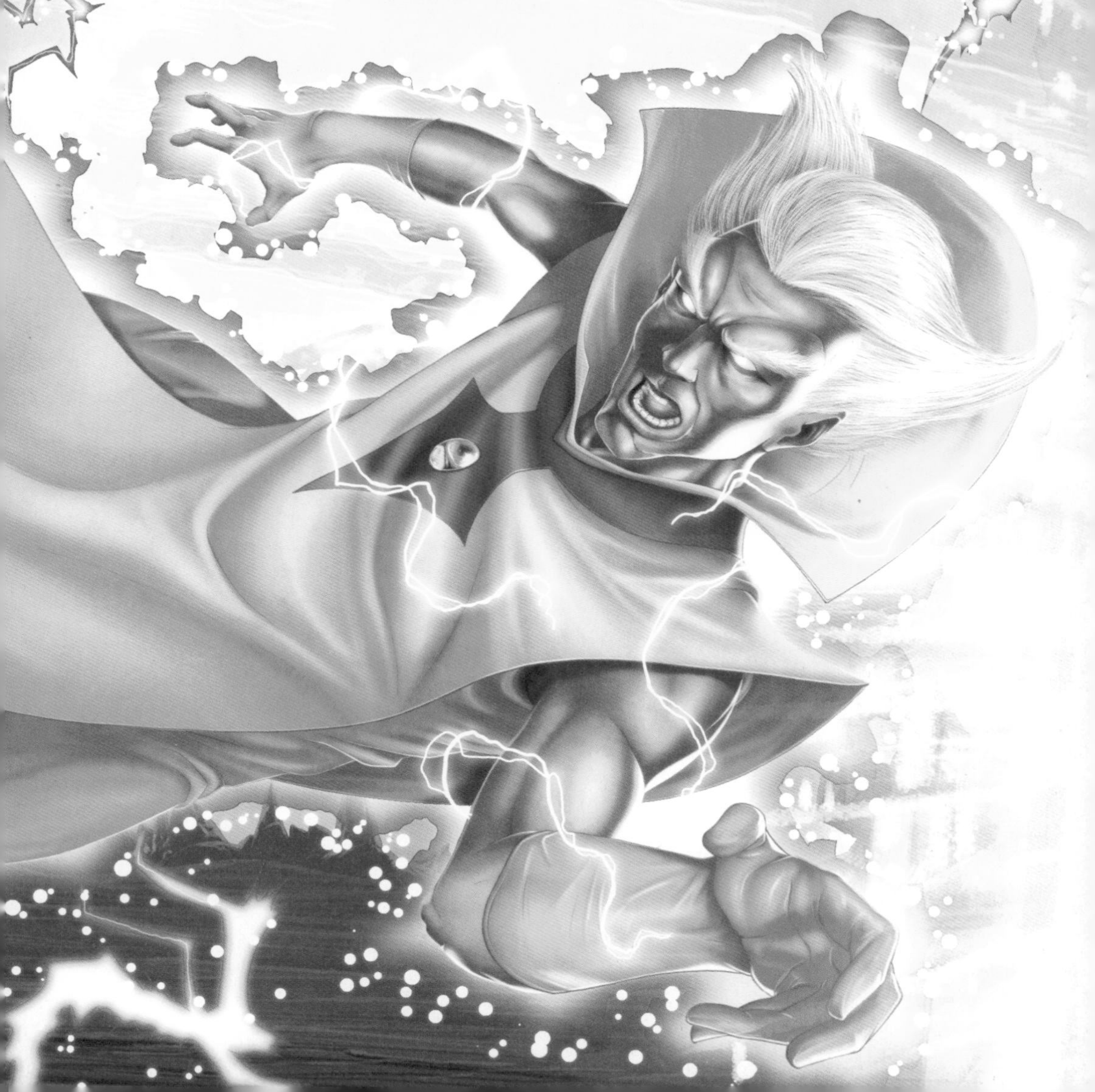

With the Moon Stone safe, the heroes headed home. "This stone is indeed powerful," Thor told the Hulk. "But the power of teamwork has saved the day!"

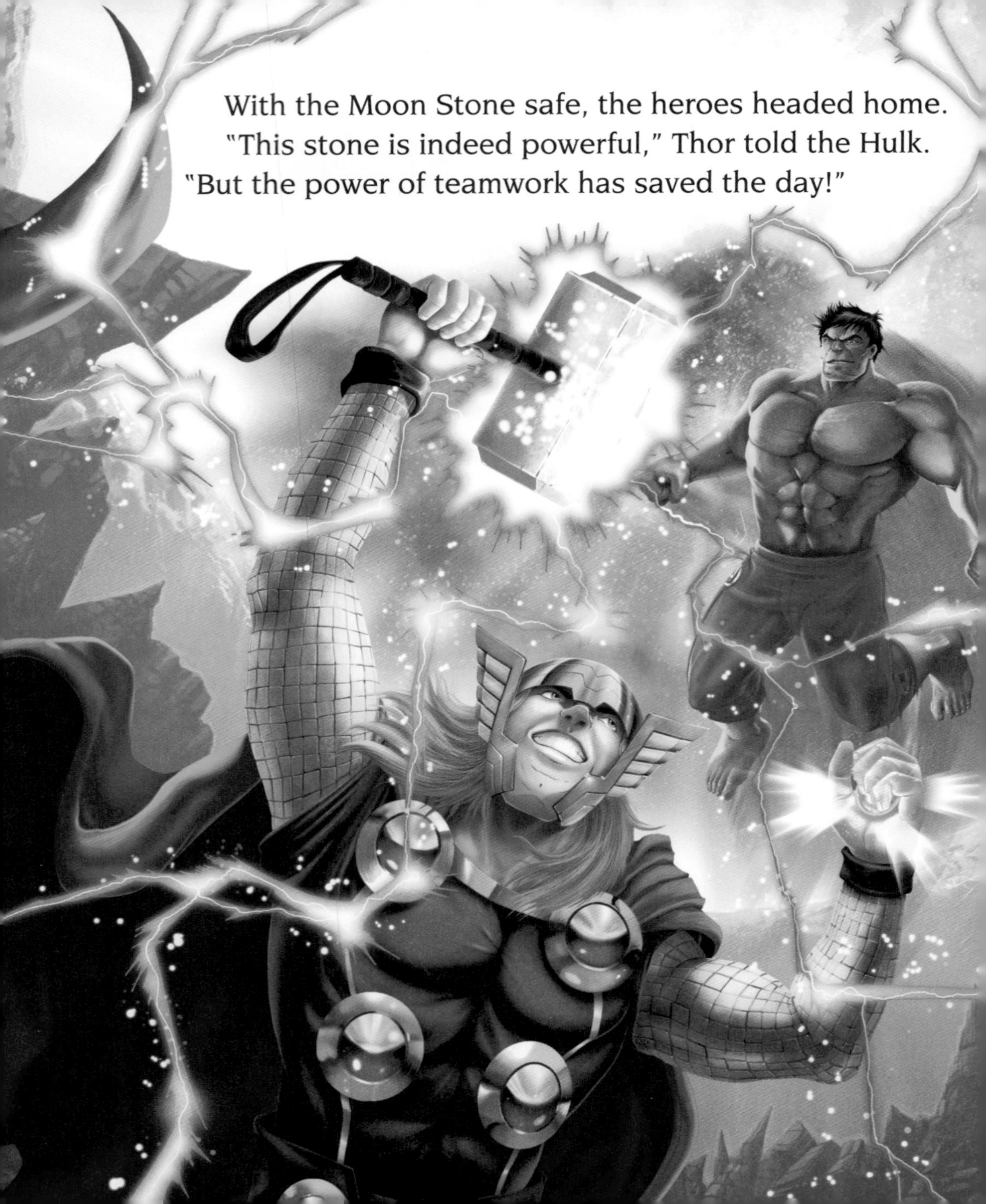